The Parents With A Sleepover Secret

DETECTIVE

DOVE

ZUNI BLUE

AMARIA & SARIEL

LONDON

THE PARENTS WITH A SLEEPOVER SECRET

For more information, please contact:

Zuni Blue at www.zuniblue.com

Print ISBN: 9781097691128

First Edition August 2013

This Edition May 2019

100 Free Gifts For You

There are 100 FREE printables waiting for you!

Certificates, bookmarks, wallpapers and more! You can choose your favourite colour: red, yellow, pink, green, orange, purple or blue.

You don't need money or an email address. Check out www.zuniblue.com to print your free gifts today.

CONTENTS

Case File No.4 1

Chapter 1 2

Chapter 2 7

Chapter 3 14

Chapter 4 28

Chapter 5 39

Chapter 6 48

Chapter 7 63

Chapter 8 76

Chapter 9 82

Chapter 10 91

Chapter 11 105

Chapter 12 115

Chapter 13 124

Chapter 14 131

Chapter 15 147

Chapter 16 157

Chapter 17 166

Chapter 18 176

Chapter 19 185

Chapter 20 191

Chapter 21 199

Chapter 22 215

Chapter 23 225

Chapter 24 239

Chapter 25 246

Chapter 26 262

Chapter 27 274

Chapter 28 280

Chapter 29 285

Chapter 30 290

Case File No.4

In London, England, you'll find Detective Inspector Mya Dove. With four years' experience on the police force, this eight-year-old is on her way to being the best police officer ever.

Yes. The best. Her mum said so.

To inspire other kids, she's sharing case files. Case No.4: The Parents With A Sleepover Secret.

Chapter 1

It was finally the Christmas holidays! The Christmas tree was up and loads of presents were packed underneath. I hoped the biggest presents were mine...

I couldn't wait to play with my dolls. I loved dressing them up like police officers. Afterwards, I'd play video games with Dad. And bake tasty chocolate cakes with Mum. Then I'd watch TV all day like my big brother Will.

"Which one should I pick first?" I wondered. "Dolls, games, cakes or TV?"

"Mya! William!" Mum yelled upstairs. "Come down, please!"

I didn't want to go downstairs because I knew exactly what she'd say: "Sorry, everyone, but I'm working on Christmas Day. Again."

Just like last year.

And the year before.

My mum was a nurse who took care of babies at the hospital. Babies are born every day, even Christmas Day, so Mum didn't get much time off.

It'd be better if babies came out in November or January instead. Then we could all spend Christmas at home and open presents.

"Detective Inspector Mya Dove, do not make me come up those stairs for you!" Mum yelled.

Uh oh…

I went straight downstairs and sat at the kitchen table. Mum was there. Dad wasn't.

When I looked at Dad's empty chair, Mum patted her lap. I sat on it and gave her a big hug.

"Where's Dad?" I asked.

"He's fine. He's coming down soon."

Mum tidied my afro hair and pulled it back into a puff. I hoped that one day my hair would be waist-length like Mum's.

"I didn't break it," I said quickly. "Or borrow it. Or dirty it."

"What on earth are you talking about?" Mum asked, raising an eyebrow. "Mya, you are not in trouble. I need to talk to you and that brother of yours. Where is he? I texted him. Phoned him. Emailed him. My goodness, he's just upstairs! What's taking so long?"

My brother was in a bad mood, and it was

his own fault. His favourite girlfriend found out about his other girlfriends. They all came over and shouted at him. It was funny! Since then, Will had been sulking in his bedroom. He only came out to pee, poo, eat, drink and fart.

Will shuffled into the kitchen with his head down. His headphones were blasting so loud I could hear the words to the song. All that noise wasn't good. I felt very sorry for his ears.

Will stuck his tongue out at me. I stuck mine out too. We both laughed.

"Where's Dad?" Will asked. "I'm really busy, you know?"

"Give him a few minutes, all right?" Mum frowned. "He needs time…"

There were tears in Mum's eyes.

When Dad walked in, I knew something was definitely wrong. His dark brown skin looked pale and his coily afro beard was very scruffy. Usually he'd be washed, shaved and dressed by now, but this time he was still in his dressing gown and slippers.

Even worse, his eyes were pink and puffy like he'd been crying a lot. I'd only seen Dad cry one time, so I knew things were REALLY bad.

"Dad?" Will asked. "What's going on?"

Dad sat at the table, his hands shaking. He bit his lip nervously and looked at Mum. She took his hand and squeezed it.

"Kids, I have something to tell you." Dad paused, his eyes on the table. "It's about your grandmother…"

Chapter 2

"What's going on?" Will asked nervously. "What's wrong with Gran?"

Dad opened his mouth to speak, but no words came out. His eyes filled with tears. I always felt really sad when Mum or Dad cried.

"William? Mya?" Dad took a hanky from his dressing gown pocket and wiped his snotty nose. "Gran, my mum, isn't very well. We're going to see her."

"It's okay, Daddy." I jumped up and gave him a big hug. Mum hugged him too. Will stood up but didn't join in. He used to hug us, but not since he became a teenager. He said teenagers were too old for group hugs.

"Is she gonna...?" Will glanced at me. "You know what I mean. Is she on her way out?"

"William, don't talk like that!" Mum snapped. If she wasn't a black person, she would've gone dark red. "We're being positive. Do the same!"

"Sorry," Will said.

"Your father and grandmother need support right now, so our holiday plans have changed. I'll call work and tell them I need time off."

"I'll stay in and help however I can," Will said. "I'll tell the guys I'm skipping the party tomorrow. I'll buy a card and gift for Gran instead."

"I'll tell the Children's Police Force I'm

busy," I said. "And I'll leave lots and lots of toys for Iam when we go to Gran's house."

Iam was Will's cat. Our neighbours always fed him when we went on holiday. Last time, they didn't leave enough food, so he caught some mice to play with. Silly Iam brought the mice into our house. We spent weeks getting them all out!

"Miss your party? Not solve cases?" Mum shook her head. "That's very sweet of you both, but you guys aren't coming to see Gran. It's Christmastime. You should be having fun with friends."

"I'm going with you," Will snapped. "Not stayin' here with Gran sick. Can't have fun knowin' she's sick."

"William," Mum's voice was louder and firmer, "you can stay with one of your *male* friends. We will be back before Christmas Eve."

"But—"

Mum turned to me.

"Mya, I called around but it was too short notice for your friends' parents. They don't have enough room or they're going on holiday. Luckily an old friend invited you over for a sleepover this week."

An old friend? Maybe it was my friend Jimmy. We'd known each other for months now. He was the coolest and most mysterious boy at school. He liked keeping secrets, so nobody knew much about him. We'd never seen his parents. His dad was a dentist, but that's all we knew.

The sleepover meant I'd be the first person at school to see inside Jimmy's house. I couldn't wait to see his police uniform! And his badge! And his baton! And—

"Their daughter was so happy to hear you were coming," Mum said. "Apparently she has picked dolls you can play with, and a teddy you can cuddle at night."

She? The "old friend" was a girl. Maybe she was my friend Libby Smith? Cool! A sleepover meant I could get to know her better.

Libby was my best friend. She was very, very shy around people and didn't say much. But she was saying more and more all the time.

Now she had five friends at school. One of them even spoke to her over the phone. I'm sure Libby was really nervous, but she managed to do it.

I was very proud of her.

"Her family is so wealthy," Mum said. "They have a swimming pool, but she doesn't swim much because it turns her hair green."

Libby had black, coily afro hair like mine. Afro hair shrinks when it's wet and might tangle, but it never changes colour.

"Her hair turns green?" I asked. "I don't understand…"

"Yes. I think it's common with blondes when they go swimming."

Blondes? The "old friend" was a blonde? The only blonde we had in class was…

Oh no. NO! NO! NO! This couldn't be happening! How could Mum do this to me? I thought she loved me!

The room was spinning. I felt sick. Mum kept talking but I didn't hear a word. I just sank into my chair and tried to catch my breath. Either that or I'd start crying like a big baby.

Calm down! I thought to myself. Calm down! Calm down! Calm down!

"Mum?" I blinked back tears. "Can I stay here with the cat?"

Mum and Dad laughed. At least I'd made

them smile.

"No," Mum said. "You're staying with your friend."

I knew exactly which blonde "friend" she was talking about. Yes, we'd been friends four years ago, but then we had a BIG argument. We hadn't liked each other since then.

Most people didn't like her because she was the meanest girl at school. She always pushed in front at lunchtime. She always took the best toys at breaktime. She always said horrible things to people.

I couldn't believe that she was ever my best friend. What was I thinking? We all make mistakes when we're young, I guess. I was only two years old when we met, and didn't realise how mean she was.

"Mum, please...Don't leave me with her!"

"Mya, go and pack your bags," Mum said. "You're staying with Angel White..."

Chapter 3

It was a cold, rainy Monday morning. I wished we could drive all the way to see Granny. Instead we were going somewhere else…

To Angel White's house.

"I think that's her place," Mum said, pointing out the window.

I saw Angel's massive house with two shiny, black cars parked outside. Mum said there was a huge swimming pool out back with a diving board! It didn't seem fair that such a mean girl could have so much cool stuff.

"We've arrived," Mum said. "I'll pull over here."

When Mum parked the car, I gave Dad the biggest hug ever. His eyes weren't so puffy anymore. I waved at Will. He nodded at me and closed his eyes.

Mum and I got out. Our eyes widened when we saw Angel's HUGE house up close. The brick walls were extra bright white with eight large windows.

"It's beautiful," Mum said. "I'd love a house like this. Maybe we'll buy one someday..."

Mum took my hand and led me up the wide garden path, white rose bushes on both sides. On the way, we passed the long driveway to the garage. It looked big enough for four cars.

At the front door, Mum rang the doorbell. Dad and Will stayed in the car. They brought Will so he'd know where I was staying.

"Is the phone on?" Mum asked. "Is it fully charged? Is the volume loud enough? I don't want you missing my calls."

I showed her the mobile. It was my first ever phone. My parents bought it so they could call me twice a day.

"We'll always be happy to hear from you," Mum said. "You can call us any time, okay?"

"Yes, Mum."

"And remember to eat all your veg at dinnertime."

"Yes, Mum."

"Follow their house rules. No naughty behaviour, is that understood?"

"Yes, Mum."

"Also, remember to clean behind your ears, pick your nose with a tissue not your finger, don't stay up late—"

She went on and on and on. Why? I already knew how to take care of myself! I wasn't two or something. I was eight, almost nine!

"...I almost forgot, always remember to pay attention when people talk to you. Did you get all that, Mya?"

"Yes, Mum."

Ding dong! Mum rang the doorbell, but nobody answered. Ding dong!

I gave her my puppy dog look.

"Please don't leave me here! I *hate* her!" I whispered. "And her friends. They're mean too."

"Hate is a very strong word," Mum said. "You are free to dislike her, but don't be so mean."

"*She's* the mean one," I said. "If you really love me, leave me with Will. I'd rather stay with him than her."

Yeah, that's how desperate I was to get away from Angel!

Mum smiled. "I know you'll miss us, baby, but you'll have so much fun with your friend."

"We're not friends!"

"You used to hold hands all the time. It was adorable."

"Six years ago!"

Ding dong!

Mum glanced at her watch and sighed. Gran lived four hours away. If Angel's parents didn't open the door soon, Mum and Dad would get stuck in traffic!

Mum pushed the doorbell again before peeking through the letterbox.

I peeked too.

Angel was in there. She was curled up on the bottom step, crying. Upstairs a man and woman were shouting at each other.

"That's Mr and Mrs White," Mum whispered. "You remember them, don't you?"

I hadn't seen Angel's parents in years. Her babysitter always took her to school and picked her up. The babysitter even went to Parents' Evening. She said Angel's parents were too busy to go.

Angel's mum looked busy today too. She was in a dark blue suit with a briefcase and folders under her arms. Jimmy said she worked in the city. They all wore suits in the city.

I didn't ever want to wear a suit. I preferred white shirts and comfy, dark trousers.

"Look, I told you about this already," Angel's mum cried. "She is coming to stay for a week. Her grandmother is poorly. I am certain Rose would take in our sweet, darling, adorable little angel if we ever asked."

"You *never* told me about this!" Angel's dad yelled. "Couldn't you tell me *before* inviting her over?"

"Well, you didn't tell before you…" It was quiet for a moment. "Anyway, I DID tell you, but you never listen. Ever! I don't know why I bother talking to you…I give up!"

Someone stomped closer to the stairs.

"Aren't you staying?" Angel's dad asked. "You're the one who invited her over, remember?"

"I can't greet them in this state," Angel's mum said. "I'm so mad I could…I could…"

Angel's mum stormed downstairs, stepped over Angel, and marched out the back door.

"Is she going back to work?" Mum whispered. "When I called earlier, she said she was finished for the day."

Angel's dad came downstairs in a dirty vest and shorts. He pulled on trousers, finger-combed his scruffy, blond beard, and pulled Angel to her feet.

"It's all right, sweet dumpling," he said. "Mummy and I just had a little, tiny argument…again. No big deal."

He took her hand and led her to the front door.

Mum quickly let go of the letterbox and we turned away, whistling to ourselves. We didn't want them to know we'd been so nosy!

The front door flew open. We turned to face them.

"Hello, Rose." Angel's dad shook Mum's hand. "My wife had an important meeting this morning. She just left. Apologies."

"It's fine, honestly," Mum said. "Thank you for taking time off work to watch the girls."

"Time off work?" Angel's dad cleared the big lump in his throat. "Yeah, usually I'd be working right now!"

Mum looked down and smiled at Angel, whose blue eyes fell to the floor.

"Long time no see," Mum said. "You are as adorable as ever."

"Thank you, Mrs Dove," Angel said. Her eyes were glued to the shiny, marble floor.

"Are you all right, Angel?" Mum asked.

Angel nodded, tears in her eyes.

"She's just upset about…" Mr White's voice went quiet. "Anyway, Mya and Angel will stay in Angel's bedroom. It'll be a fun, girly sleepover!"

"Yay," Angel and I grumbled.

"Angel, take Mya upstairs and show her your bedroom. Let her choose which side of the bed she wishes to sleep on."

Angel led me upstairs to her bedroom. She

pushed open the door and let me go in first. That was a big surprise! She always pushed in front at school.

"Angel, I don't know why you're acting so strange, but you won't trick me. I know you're up to no good!" My jaw dropped when I saw her bedroom. "Whoa…"

The bedroom was massive! You could fit three of my bedroom in hers. She had a big waterbed, a large hammock on her own balcony, and a playhouse that had working lights and running water.

But there was one thing I hated about the room: it was bright pink. The walls, carpet, bed cover, pillows, chair, cushions, lampshades and even the door were light pink. It was like someone had painted my eyes pink! Yuck!

Besides the pink, I could've stayed in her room forever. All those dolls, clothes, shoes, and no one to share them with. All mine...I mean *hers*.

But I couldn't look too excited. She loved when people got jealous. Any minute now, she'd start showing off.

She'd say her bedroom was prettier than mine. She'd say her swimming pool was better than my paddling pool. She'd say her driveway was bigger than my whole house.

And, honestly, she'd be right. I'd gladly swap my house and Will for her place. Her house could eat mine for breakfast and leave lots of space for lunch.

"Go on," I said. "Say it, you show-off!"

Angel went to the balcony and sat in the hammock. I followed her.

"Just say it!" I crossed my arms in a huff. I didn't want her to think I was jealous, but...I was. Just a little bit. "Say your bedroom is a billion times better than mine! Go on. Just say it."

She shrugged.

"Go on," I said again. "Just get it over with. Say it. Say your house is bigger than mine."

She shrugged again, watching the road.

I couldn't believe it. For the first time in years, Angel White wasn't being mean. We'd known each other since nursery. She hadn't been nice since then.

But today she was *distracted* by something.

I followed her eyes to my mum's car. Dad was dragging my suitcase into the house. Mum was chatting to Angel's dad. Will stayed in the car, playing games on his phone.

"Mya, may I ask you a question?"

"Okay, I guess."

"Do your parents fight a lot?"

"Only when Dad leaves the toilet seat up. Or when Mum buys too many shoes."

"I thought so," Angel said. "That's normal Mum and Dad fighting."

She sighed heavily.

After all the mean things she'd said and done to me, I should've just walked away. I didn't because a good police officer listens to people. Even mean people like Angel.

"Angel, tell me what's wrong."

"Promise to keep it a secret?"

I nodded.

"Mya, something terrible is going to happen." She grabbed me by the arms and pulled me closer. "I can't believe it!"

"Go on, tell me!"

"I thought it was something bad like my mum having a baby."

"Why's that bad?"

"Because I don't want to share my parents. Why should I? I am their princess. We don't *need* another princess." She tucked her blonde curls behind her ears. "If they have a baby, it will cry all the time. Babies are annoying."

"You said something bad is gonna happen. If it's not a new baby, what is it?"

"Mya," she whispered, "I think my parents are going to divorce…"

Chapter 4

Were Angel's parents really divorcing? I couldn't imagine my parents not being in love anymore.

"Are you sure they're divorcing?" I asked. "Did they tell you?"

"Yes, I'm sure," she snapped. "No, they didn't tell me about the divorce. My parents always keep bad news a secret, just like the time my dad got a pay cut. Because we had less money, we only went on holiday four times that year."

Four times! My family hadn't been on

holiday since...I couldn't even remember.

"If they won't say they're divorcing, how'd you know they are?" I asked.

"I looked online, duh! I found an article called *5 Signs Your Parents Might Be Divorcing*." Angel wiped tears from her eyes. "One sign is them looking different. Did you see Daddy? He doesn't shave anymore!"

"My mum doesn't shave her legs every day," I said. "She said it's tee...ted..."

"Tedious."

"Yeah, it's boring."

"But Dad never found shaving boring before. Why now?"

Angel went back inside and sat on her waterbed. I sat down too. I'd never been on a waterbed before. It was fun bobbing up and down on it. Just like being on a boat.

"Mya, you have to help me!"

"No way," I said. "You're the meanest girl

at school. You'd *never* help me!"

"But we used to be best friends…"

That was true.

Many, many years ago, when we were only three years old, Angel and I were best friends. We always played in the sandpit together, ate lunch together, and even went to naptimes together.

Then one day she went into the sandpit and threw sand on a girl's hair. I couldn't believe my best friend could be so mean. I thought maybe she was just in a bad mood.

The next day, she squirted orange juice into a boy's face. She did it because he took her favourite naptime spot. The boy cried until his mum came to get him.

I never found out why Angel became such a mean person, but it didn't matter now. I wouldn't help mean people like her.

"Angel, you're on your own," I said. "I'm

not helping you."

Angel curled into a ball and cried.

I shrugged. I'd seen her fake cry loads of times. She did it to get her own way.

A minute later, she sat up and gave me a mean look. I couldn't see any tears. Her eyes were completely dry.

"Okay, fine," Angel said. "How much do you want?"

"What do you mean?"

"Daddy cut my allowance, so money is low right now. That's why I only have ten thousand pounds in my savings account. Is that enough?"

Wow. Ten thousand pounds! If I solved the case, I'd get all that money. I could buy lots of medicine for Gran so she'd get better quicker.

But I couldn't take money from such a mean person. It didn't feel right. She'd probably done mean things to get that money. By taking it, would I be mean too?

"Keep your money."

"What?" she gasped. "Are you crazy? Ten thousand pounds can buy lots and lots of things."

And a lot of grapes too.

I loved eating juicy, green grapes. I could eat them for breakfast, lunch and dinner. Maybe for snacks too.

But how could I eat those tasty grapes knowing I bought them with Angel's money? They wouldn't taste so good...

"No thanks," I said. "Ask someone else for help."

Angel's dad brought in my suitcase and placed it by the door. He patted us both on the head before hurrying out.

"I love my daddy," Angel said. "I want my parents to be together forever."

"I'm not helping someone mean like you, okay? No way!"

Angel reached into her bright pink dress pocket and pulled out a shiny, pink mobile phone. She quickly pressed some buttons and held the phone to her ear.

"Who're you calling?" I asked, a bad feeling in my stomach.

She stared right past me.

"Angel, tell me!"

"Oh, hello. Is this the Children's Police Force? The one at Lucia Baker Primary School?" Angel looked at me, her eyes narrowing. "Yes, well, I'd like to speak with the police girls' boss, please."

My secret boss? The boss I met in the girls' bathroom at school? She always stayed hidden in the toilet stall. I didn't know her name or what she looked like. How did Angel get her phone number?

"Hello, is this…" Angel lowered her voice so I couldn't hear the name. "Hello again! How are you?"

Was Angel friends with my boss? My boss was as mean as Angel. I guess mean people liked being friends with each other.

"Well, I have a big problem with one of your police officers," Angel said. "Mya Dove. Yes, that one."

Uh oh…

"I asked her for help, but she said no." Angel pretended to cry. "I don't know why she's being so mean to me. I thought police officers were nice."

How did she know about the Children's Police Force? How did she know I was a police officer? How many people at school knew? I thought it was a secret!

Maybe I'd shown too many people my badge, handcuffs, helmet, and other police stuff. Oops! My secret police job wasn't so secret anymore…

"No, I don't want Detective Dove to be told off," Angel said. "I want her to be made redundant."

Redundant? What did that mean?

"No, I mean I want you to let her go…"

Go where? Back home? I didn't understand what she was saying.

"Oh for goodness sake!" Angel cried. "I want you to take away her badge, handcuffs and case files…I want her fired!"

Angel handed me the phone.

"It's for you."

I put the phone to my ear.

"Detective Inspector Mya Dove," my secret boss snapped, "you are NOT a police officer anymore. After the holidays, give us your badge and handcuffs. You are NOT allowed to solve any more cases. You DO

NOT work for the Children's Police Force anymore. From now on you'll be called…Mya Dove. No more Detective Inspector for you!"

I dropped the phone and it landed on my foot, but it didn't hurt because I was already hurting inside.

I'd just lost my job. I wasn't in the Children's Police Force anymore. When I got older, the police station wouldn't work with me. They'd think I was a mean police officer who didn't help people.

If I wasn't a police officer anymore, what else could I be?

When I was two, I wanted to be a frog, but I couldn't do that now. I didn't know how to be a frog! And I didn't want to live in the garden. There were massive spiders out there. Massive! The big, hairy ones that swim when you try to wash them down the drain.

But becoming a police officer changed everything. I didn't have to worry about evil spiders anymore. When they showed up, I flashed my badge. They ran away scared that I'd arrest them.

If I couldn't be a frog or a police officer, what else could I be?

When I was three, I wanted to be an astronaut. I stuck an upside-down fishbowl over my head and pretended it was a helmet. Then I took it off and jumped on my trampoline. I'd bounce around just like the astronauts in space.

But then I realised something terrible: I couldn't buy any grapes in space. I wasn't sure if I could grow them either. If I stayed in space, I could never eat grapes again. I couldn't live without them, so I couldn't be an astronaut.

That's why being a police officer was the

best job for me. The Children's Police Force promised to pay me loads of grapes. All I had to do was solve cases at school.

But now I'd never solve cases again.

I can't believe it, I thought to myself. My dream of being the best police officer in the world is over…

Chapter 5

"Hello?" my secret boss yelled down the mobile. "Did you drop the phone, Mya?"

I rushed to pick it up.

"Please don't take away my police job," I said. "It means a lot to me."

"You can always get another job."

"But I want this one!"

"Then prove it," my boss said. "Sometimes we have to do jobs we don't like. That's part of growing up. You're almost nine years old. Time to grow up!"

I had no choice. If I didn't help Angel, I'd

be kicked out of the Children's Police Force.

"I'll help her," I said. "So, can I have my job back?"

"Yes…but you'd better do a good job!"

"I will," I said. "I promise you both!"

"Angel will tell you all about the case. Listen to her. Help her. Do your job!"

"Who left this downstairs?" a woman yelled over the phone. "Answer me, young lady!"

"I have to go," my boss whispered. "Speak to you later!"

She hung up.

Angel snatched the mobile and tossed it on to the bed. She sighed happily, a smirk on her face. She liked getting her own way.

"Tell me how to help," I mumbled.

"Sorry, can't hear you!" She grinned.

"How can I help you?" I said louder.

"Find out if my parents are really

divorcing. If they are, stop them!"

Angel rushed over to a chest of drawers. She pushed aside some socks and tights, revealing a bright pink piggy bank. I peered through the coin slot at the money inside.

"There's at least fifty pounds in there," she said. "I have ten thousand more in my bank account."

I only had five pounds in my piggy bank...

"Get some officers over here to help," she ordered. "You aren't smart enough to do this on your own."

That really made me mad! I gritted my teeth and clenched my fists, but didn't say anything. If I made her angry, I'd lose my job as a police officer again.

But she wouldn't get away with being so mean to me. I WAS smart enough to stop the divorce myself. I didn't need anyone else's help.

Besides, I didn't want to share ten thousand pounds with anyone but my family. I could buy lots of medicine for Granny. When she was better, we could both buy lots of juicy, green grapes to eat.

Angel got her mobile from the bed and shoved it into my hands. Then she stood there, watching me closely.

"Call for back-up!" she spat. "Quickly! I don't have all day, you know."

She wanted me to call some Children's Police Force officers for help, but I wanted to solve the case by myself. That way I wouldn't have to share the money.

"Mya, if you don't call for back-up right now…"

"Okay, okay! I'll do it."

I *pretended* to dial Jimmy's number, but I was really calling our house phone. Nobody was home, so it kept ringing and ringing.

"Hello, Jimmy," I said, pretending he'd answered. "Can you help me with a case?"

I stopped talking so it looked like he was speaking.

"You're too busy?" I said sadly. "Oh well. Say hello to Santa for me. Bye!"

I pretended to put the phone down and call someone else.

"Hello, um, Nicky—"

"Nicky?" Angel's eyes narrowed. "There isn't anyone called Nicky in our class."

"Quiet!" I hissed. "Nicky, hi…What? You're in Australia? It'll take a day to get here? But we must start the investigation ASAP!"

"Try someone else!" Angel snapped.

I pretended to call another officer.

"Hello? I can't hear you! Hello?" I hung up. "Tracey's at a Christmas party. You know how some ten-year-olds are. All they do is party."

Angel grabbed the phone and threw it out the window. I stood there with my mouth wide open. That phone must have cost lots of money, but she didn't care.

"Your phone…"

"I'll get another one," she snapped. "How can every officer be busy at the same time? The Children's Police Force sucks!"

"Then why didn't you call the adult police instead?" I muttered.

"I DID! I tried to call the REAL police, but they put the phone down on me. Very rude!" Angel picked up a teddy bear and threw it across the room. "They said it was naughty to call them unless it was a real emergency, but this IS a real emergency! My parents might be divorcing and someone must stop them!"

That someone would be me.

With ten thousand pounds, I could buy medicine and hundreds, no, *thousands* of green grapes.

But first, I needed to solve the case.

"Angel, tell me about your parents," I said. "And give me the divorce signs article you found."

She handed it over.

"What's the first sign of a divorce?" I asked, looking down the page. "It says sleeping in different rooms."

Angel nodded, a tear in her eye.

"My dad sleeps downstairs now. He said it's because Mum snores. Her snoring doesn't mean he has to sleep downstairs, though. Why can't he stay upstairs in our guest bedrooms? We've got three!"

"I don't know," I said. "Why do you think he sleeps downstairs?"

"Because he doesn't want to be close to Mum anymore." Her blue eyes fell to the fluffy carpet. "Maybe he doesn't want to be near me either."

"Or maybe, like he told you, he sleeps downstairs because your mum snores."

"How do we know he's telling the truth?" she asked. "Parents lie sometimes."

"Have they lied to you before?"

"Yes," she said. "Last year, they promised to buy me a gerbil. Instead, they bought me a pony. I was so upset. I like ponies, but I LOVE gerbils!"

Poor little Angel, I thought. It must've been so hard having a sweet, beautiful pony to ride…

"Tomorrow morning, we'll find out if your mum snores. Then we'll know if your dad sleeps downstairs because she snores or because they're divorcing."

I took out my mobile and set the alarm. On Tuesday, we'd wake up nice and early to catch Mrs White snoring.

"So, we'll sneak into Mum's room and see if she snores?"

"Yep," I said. "Simple as that."

Well, that's what I thought anyway, but I was wrong. Our trip to Mrs White's room wouldn't be simple. Soon we'd discover a shocking secret that would change Angel's life forever...

Chapter 6

At three in the morning, the alarm clock went off. I pressed the snooze button, rolled over and went back to sleep.

At four in the morning, the alarm went off again. I wanted to turn it off again, but then I remembered we had an important job to do!

Today we'd find out if Angel's mum snored really loud. If she did, Mr White couldn't sleep next to her. That's why he slept downstairs by himself.

I rolled over and shook Angel. She slapped my hands away and went back to sleep.

"Angel, wake up," I whispered. "We've got work to do."

"Later," she mumbled. "It's too early!"

I couldn't sit around waiting for her. I had to reach Mrs White's bedroom before she woke up.

I jumped out of bed and tiptoed across the soft carpet. It made my footsteps very, very quiet.

Good, I thought. She won't hear me coming.

I opened the bedroom door a crack and peeked into the upstairs hallway. There were so many doors. That's when I realised my mistake: I didn't know which room Angel's mum was in.

There were seven rooms. I went to the one beside Angel's bedroom and pressed my ear against the door. I couldn't hear anyone, so I went inside.

It was a bathroom. A HUGE one. There was a pink toothbrush and strawberry toothpaste on the sink. A pink flannel and rubber duckies were sitting by the bath.

I wonder whose pink bathroom this is, I thought to myself. I wonder…

Next door was another bathroom, but it was half the size. It didn't look like anyone used this one.

Where is Mrs White's bedroom? I thought. I'll try next door.

I did find a bedroom, but it wasn't Mrs White's. This room was full of loads and loads of toys. There were dolls, dollhouses, teddies, and a car big enough to get inside. I jumped in but it wouldn't turn on. It was covered in dust, so I got out and dusted myself off.

I don't have time to play around, I thought. Get moving!

I closed the door quietly and went to the next room. It was packed with hundreds of pretty dresses and shiny, new shoes. No one could sleep in this bedroom either because there was no space.

The next bedroom was even more crowded. I could barely get the door open. To squeeze inside, I had to hold my breath.

When I got inside, it was hard to see what everything was. My dad would've called it all junk. Plain, old junk. There were broken toys, clothes with holes in them, shoeboxes with a shoe missing, and dust everywhere.

The thick, dusty air made it hard to breathe. All the dust kept sneaking up my nose. It was so ticklish! I covered my mouth with my nightie, just in case I sneezed really loudly.

Wow, I thought. Maybe *this* is why Mr White sleeps downstairs. There's no free bedroom up here.

I squeezed out of the room and stopped to catch my breath. It'd been so dusty and crowded in there. Being back in the hallway felt so good.

Let's try next door, I thought. If Mrs White is in there, I hope she's still asleep!

I quietly knocked twice. No answer. I knocked again, just to be sure. I couldn't just walk in if she was awake. She'd start asking questions and figure out I was investigating their divorce.

Slowly I opened the door a little. The smell of strong perfume smacked me in the face. I held my nose and closed the door.

"It's honey, rosemary and peppermint," a voice said behind me.

I jumped from fright and fell over. I looked back and found Angel standing over me. She rubbed her eyes and yawned.

"Mum says I'm too young for perfume," she said quietly. "I am NOT too young. I am nine. Daddy lets me wear it when Mum isn't home."

"You're late," I snapped.

"So? I can be late to an investigation because I'm not a police officer, you are. I am a princess, Daddy says, and a princess can show up any time she likes."

She stuck out her tongue.

Stay calm and think of Granny, I told myself. And think of the juicy grapes. And the money to buy lots of Christmas presents.

"I'm going in," I whispered. "You coming?"

She nodded.

I turned the door knob and went inside.

Angel's parents had a very boring bedroom. The walls, ceiling and fluffy carpet were all white. So were the wardrobes, drawers, dressing table, chair and the huge bed.

The only part that wasn't white was a family photo hanging over the bed. The picture was taken when Angel was a cute, chubby little baby. Her parents looked so much younger, and a lot happier.

"I want my old life back," Angel whispered. "Back when my parents still loved each other."

"If they're divorcing, we can stop them!"

"What if we can't?" She turned away from me. "Just listen…"

We stood in silence for a moment.

"Listen to what?" I asked, cupping a hand to my ear. "I can't hear anything but us talking."

"Exactly," she said, "Daddy told me he sleeps downstairs because Mum snores too loud. We can see she doesn't snore at all, so why does he really sleep downstairs?"

She was right. Mrs White was under the duvet. I could barely hear or see her. The bed covers slowly moved up and down when she breathed, but there was no snoring.

Angel went to the dressing table and pulled open a drawer. She reached inside and lifted out a thin laptop. It was so light she could hold it with one hand.

"Let's check her computer," she whispered. "The other day, there was something she didn't want me to see. She closed the laptop when I walked over."

"We shouldn't snoop through other people's things."

"But my parents go through MY things all the time!"

"Parents can go through our things because they paid for them. That's what my brother said anyway…"

"Well, he's wrong," she said. "It's *my* house, so I can look wherever I like."

Angel turned on the laptop and typed in the password. Her fingers moved so quickly they were a blur. I couldn't imagine being able to type that fast.

"You should've turned around," she said. "It's rude to look at other people's passwords."

"Then you must've been rude too."

"What?"

"It's your mum's password, not yours," I said. "You must've been watching when she typed it in."

"Whatever, loser!" she spat.

Angel opened the internet browser on the laptop. When she clicked the History tab, it showed the websites her mum went on in the past month.

"I can't see anything about a divorce," I

whispered. "Keep looking."

Next, we looked at Mrs White's Search History. It included words like business contracts, legal agreements, lawyers, accountants, project managers, national corporations, international corporations, and…houses.

"Houses?" we both cried.

Mrs White sat up. Luckily she wore a big eye mask or she would've seen us.

"Drew, is that you?" she asked. "I heard you typing."

Angel and I kept perfectly still. We didn't say a word.

"Put my laptop away when you're done," she said. "And put it on charge."

Mrs White let out a massive yawn and went back to sleep. I peeked over the bed. All I could see was her hair bonnet poking out from under the covers.

"We've got to go," I said. "We might get caught next time!"

"I'm not going," Angel snapped. "Not until I'm done."

She clicked the link to a house website. It showed lots of houses people could buy. Her eyes widened when she scrolled down the page.

"Mya, the houses are so…so…*small*!"

The houses were the same size as my house, but much smaller than Angel's. My house had three bedrooms, not five. We had one bathroom, not three. Our house didn't come with a swimming pool or massive driveway.

"Mya, look at the tiny houses!"

"They're normal-sized," I said.

"My playhouse is bigger than that house. And look at that one! It doesn't have a utility room. Where do they put the washing machine?"

"In the kitchen, silly!" I said. "I thought everyone knew that."

"Does your cleaner wash your clothes in the kitchen?"

"I don't have a cleaner."

"So who cleans your stuff?"

"My mum," I said. "Anyway, why was your mum looking at houses?"

"I know why," she said sadly. "When parents get a divorce, one of them moves out."

"So your mum is…"

"Moving out."

Angel quietly sobbed in her hands. I put my arm around her and just held her. It felt strange hugging her. She was still a mean person, but she used to be my friend. We used to hug all the time at nursery.

"Angel, maybe she's not moving out.

Maybe she's…Or maybe they're…It doesn't mean…"

"You're right," she said.

"I am?"

"Looking at houses doesn't mean she's leaving us. Maybe she's buying us another house. Then I'll have more bedrooms and even more toys!"

Angel closed the laptop and put it away. She wasn't crying anymore.

"Let's check on your dad," I whispered. "We'll go back to bed before they wake up."

We sneaked out of the bedroom and tiptoed downstairs.

Mr White was in the living room, snoring on the three-seater sofa. Beside him was a coffee table with an open laptop on it. The screen was off. Next to the laptop were newspapers scattered across the table.

Under the table was Prince, Angel's white

poodle. His narrow eyes were watching me closely.

I crept over to Angel's dad and waited to see if he woke up. He didn't.

Prince flashed his teeth at me.

"Calm down," Angel whispered. "It's okay. I don't like her either."

I stuck my tongue out at her. Prince didn't like that. He edged closer, growling.

"Now you've upset him," she said. "Poor baby."

Angel tiptoed over and pulled Prince away. He kept looking at me, showing his sharp teeth. I showed mine back.

Suddenly Prince jumped at me and started barking. The noise made Mr White jump from fright. He jumped again when he saw me.

"Mya?" He rubbed his half-open eyes. "What're you doing down here?"

Uh oh…

Chapter 7

Angel and her dog ducked behind the sofa and kept perfectly still. I knew they weren't coming to help me.

I was on my own.

"Mya," Mr White said, "I asked what you're doing down here?" He rubbed his baggy eyes. "Are you peckish? Or thirsty? Or maybe you had a nightmare?"

"Yes."

"Yes to which one?"

"All of them," I said. "I had a nightmare. I woke up. I felt hungry and thirsty."

"Mya, is something wrong?" he asked.

Mr White turned on the lamp by the sofa and patted the spot beside him. I didn't sit down because it wasn't time to be friendly. I meant serious police business. He wasn't just my babysitter anymore. He was an important part of this divorce case.

He yawned without covering his mouth, which is very rude!

"I think I know what the matter is…"

"You do?" I gulped.

"Poor girl. You're worried about your grandmother, aren't you? Don't worry. She'll get better soon."

Of course she would! She'd promised to live to a hundred years old.

"I'm not here about Granny," I said.

"So what're you here for?" he asked.

I reached into my nightie pocket and pulled out my shiny police badge. It had my badge number on it: 180289. First, Mr White looked very impressed, then a little worried.

"Mr White, I have some questions. You can call a lawyer if you like, but you'll have to pay him yourself."

"A lawyer?" His eyes narrowed. "Sorry, what's this about?"

He was doing the "I haven't done anything wrong" act, but he wasn't fooling me!

"Mr White—"

"Call me Andrew."

"No, thank you."

Police officers use surnames only. First names sound too friendly. We weren't friends. I was an officer and he was a divorce suspect!

"Mr White, I have some questions."

"Then let's talk."

"Mr White, someone told me you stopped shaving. Is this true?"

"Someone told you this? Was it Bonnie or Angel?" He gently prodded my nose. "Or maybe you're making this up!"

"Is it true? Have you stopped shaving forever?"

"Not necessarily forever, but yes. I get a bit fed up with shaving my beard sometimes." He ruffled his fuzzy, blond beard. "I might let it grow all big and fluffy like Santa's. Your father's beard is nice too. I'll ask him for tips next time I see him."

Why did he bring up my dad's beard? Because he wanted to get on my good side. Well, it didn't work. It just made me more suspicious...

"Does Mrs White like beards?"

His eyes shifted away.

"No," he grumbled. "Too bad."

He didn't care what Mrs White thought about his beard. Maybe because they were divorcing soon?

Angel slowly peeked over her dad's shoulder. Her eyes shifted from me to the newspapers on the table. Then she sank back down into the shadows.

I leaned over and saw jobs circled in the newspaper. Mr White realised I was being nosy, so he grabbed the newspapers and folded them up.

"Why're you looking for jobs?" I asked.

"Because I would like to earn more money," he said, sweat trickling down his forehead. "Why not have another job?"

That didn't make sense to me. My mum and dad both had one job each. They didn't have time for loads of jobs.

I only had time for two jobs (student and police officer) because I could solve cases in my free time. When I was older, I'd only have time for one job: being a police officer.

"What's your job, Mr White?"

"I was…I am an Office Manager now. I help all the lawyers, including my wife." He glanced down at the newspapers. "I'd like to have two jobs."

"Why?"

"Because then we can have more money. I'll buy Angel even more toys, sweets and maybe another cute doggy."

I remembered the three spare bedrooms upstairs. They were packed with Angel's old toys and clothes. I couldn't understand why Mr White wanted to buy her more things. She already had too much!

"Is your job like my mum's job?" I asked. "She works all night. Or is your job like my dad's? He works when he likes."

Mr White's eyes lit up.

"Your father is self-employed. That means he is his own boss. No one tells him what to do…I love the sound of that."

"Why? Don't you like your job?"

"Of course I do."

"Then get another job at your workplace," I said. "They'll give you more money, right? Like a promotion!"

His eyes widened in surprise.

"You're a very smart girl," he said, picking up the TV remote. "Any other questions, Mya? I'm missing the news."

The news repeats all day, so he wasn't missing anything! It was just an excuse to stop talking. Too bad! The questions stop when the police officer says so.

"Just one more thing, Mr White…" I left a very long pause to make him really nervous. Police officers did that on TV shows. "Someone said you stopped putting the toilet seat down? You know Mrs White hates when you leave it up."

"No comment," he said. "We're done here, I think. That's a very personal question."

"No, we're not done yet!" I snapped. "I have *more* questions."

"Look, Officer Mya, an interrogation ends when the suspect requests legal representation…which is exactly what I am doing now. I want a lawyer and will not say any more until my lawyer gets here."

I wasn't sure if that was the law or not. I couldn't call Mum or Dad to ask because it was still very early in the morning!

"Where's your lawyer?" I asked. "I can wait until he gets here."

"Not he, *she*," he said. "She, my wife, is still asleep. I will not wake her up. You'll just have to wait a couple of hours until she comes down."

"But—"

"But nothing, Officer Mya." He pinched my cheeks. "Aw, so cute. Now go to bed."

He turned back to the TV and flipped through the channels.

I wasn't very happy about him pinching my cheeks like that. I wasn't just some little kid. I was a police officer that took care of Britain.

Something else bothered me too.

I thought people divorced when they didn't love each other anymore. If Mrs White didn't love Mr White, why was she his lawyer? Why was she still helping him?

Before I left the room, I noticed something peeking out from behind the sofa cushions. It looked like Angel's silky pillowcase, but this pillow was white instead of bright pink.

"Mr White, why are you sleeping downstairs?"

"Because I like to fall asleep with the TV on. Mrs White prefers silence before bed."

"Really?" I said. "Are you sure that's why you're down here?"

"What other reason could there be?"

He'd told Angel he slept downstairs because of Mrs White's snoring. Now he was telling me something different. He kept telling lies to hide the truth.

What was the truth? Did he sleep downstairs because they were divorcing? I wasn't sure. Sometimes my dad slept downstairs when Mum was angry at him. It happened last Christmas when he bought her a toolbox instead of perfume. Dad had to sleep downstairs every night until New Year's Eve.

All parents argued sometimes. Silly fights

were over things like checking mobiles at the dinner table. Other fights were more serious, like whether or not to ask for directions in the car.

Were Angel's parents fighting over something silly or something very serious? I wouldn't find out right now because Mr White was done answering my questions.

I turned to leave but remembered something important: Angel was still hiding behind the sofa!

"Mr White?" I asked.

"Yes," he muttered.

"Can I have some water, please?"

When he went to the kitchen, Angel slipped out to the hallway. I waited for Mr White and drank my water before leaving.

In the hallway, Angel was sitting on the stairs with tears streaming down her cheeks. I sat beside her and patted her back.

"Mya, do you know why he's looking for jobs?"

I shook my head.

"Mum is looking for houses because she wants to move out. Dad is looking for jobs because if Mum moves out, we'll have less money. I won't be able to buy new toys every month."

Every single month? I only got new toys at Christmas, my birthday, and if I did really well at school.

"Daddy wants another job so we can still be rich. He's doing it for me because I'm his princess."

It sounded like Angel was right. Mrs White wanted to leave because they were divorcing. She'd take her money and go. Mr White needed another job so he could still buy lots of things for Angel.

I took out the divorce list and crossed off

the first sign of a divorce: sleeping in different rooms.

Were they really getting a divorce? Maybe. Maybe not. Mr White hadn't been very helpful at all, so I needed to talk to Mrs White. She was still asleep. Too bad. It was time to wake her up...

Chapter 8

"It's time to wake your mum up," I whispered to Angel. "Let's go!"

We tiptoed upstairs and stopped outside her parents' bedroom door.

It was still very early, but I needed to see Mrs White. I could've waited until later that morning, but Mr White might warn her first.

I pressed my ear against the bedroom door and heard Angel's mum whispering to someone. I knocked and the whispering stopped.

Mrs White was *pretending* to sleep, but she

didn't fool me. I kept knocking until the door opened.

"Hello, Mrs…"

A woman I didn't know stood there. She wore a bright yellow dressing gown and fluffy slippers. They looked very comfortable on her feet. I peered into the bedroom but Mrs White wasn't there.

"Hello," I said. "Could I speak to Mrs White, please?"

"Mya, darling, it's me."

"Hello," I said again. "Who are you?"

"Mrs White."

Impossible! I rubbed my eyes and looked again. She had Mrs White's soft voice, but everything else was different.

Angel's mum had straight, blonde hair that stopped at her shoulders. This woman had curly, brown hair that reached her waist.

Angel's mum had big, bright blue eyes.

This woman had narrow, dark green eyes.

Angel's mum had smooth skin and no spots on her face. This woman had some wrinkles like my gran and moles like my dad.

Both women were very pretty, but they definitely weren't the same person…right?

The woman stepped aside and pointed at the open wardrobe behind her. Sitting between a brush and hairspray was a blonde wig. Beside it was a box of blue contact lenses. Next to the box was a make-up set.

"I know I look a little different," she said.

"Yeah. You look a *little* different…"

Part of me still wondered if the real Mrs White was hiding somewhere. I was very tempted to check under the bed and behind the clothes in the wardrobe…

"Anyway, good morning, Mya." She didn't sound very happy to see me. "What time is it?"

"I don't know."

She glanced at something in her dressing gown pocket.

"It's not even five o'clock yet." She yawned without covering her mouth. Very rude! "Can we talk about this when the sun comes up? Say around seven or eight?"

"It can't wait," I said. "Angel needs to talk to you."

"Angel?" she asked, looking confused. "Where is she?"

I looked back but nobody was there. At the end of the hallway was Angel's door. It was open a little, a blue eye peeking out.

"Is this about my husband not shaving?" she asked.

"Yes, how'd you know?"

"A lucky guess," she said. "Anyway, sometimes men don't shave."

"But you don't like his beard, do you?"

She looked away.

"Of course I do," she mumbled.

Mr White was looking different. Mrs White was looking different too. I took out the list of divorce signs Angel had printed. Changing their look was one of the signs!

So far there's two signs they're divorcing, I thought. This isn't looking good…

"So why're you fighting all the time?"

"Fighting is a strong word," she said. "I prefer to call it bickering."

"Okay, why are you bickering all the time? You shouldn't be unless…" I lowered my voice. "Unless Mr White did something that made you *very* angry."

She crouched down until we were eye to eye. Her voice lowered. Now I could barely hear her.

"He told you, didn't he?" Her eyes widened. "You can't tell Angel yet! She'll be devastated!"

"Mr White didn't tell me anything," I said. "I figured it out myself."

"Does Angel know?"

"She doesn't know for sure," I said. "She asked me to find out what's going on."

"Oh dear," Mrs White said, her face turning pale. "Our little princess knows the truth. My poor darling must be so distraught..."

I couldn't believe it! Angel had been right all along. Her parents were getting a divorce.

"Are you sure about this?" I asked. "Is this really happening?"

"Happening?" Mrs White shook her head. "My dear, it's already happened..."

Chapter 9

I couldn't believe it. It *sounded* like Angel's parents had already divorced. Mrs White didn't actually *say* they'd divorced, probably because it was really hard to talk about.

"Whose idea was it? His or yours?"

"His, of course." Her eyes narrowed. "Anyway, does it matter now? What's done is done."

She stepped back into the bedroom and yawned again.

"Well, we'd better go back to bed," she said. "You must be terribly tired."

"But we've still got to talk about the…you know." I wasn't sure if I should say the word divorce or not. Would it make her cry? "I know this must be very hard for you. I'm here to help, okay?"

Sometimes you have to play nice with a suspect, especially when they're sleepy and haven't had their coffee yet. My mum is like a zombie if she skips her morning coffee. Dad's the same, but with tea.

To be extra nice, I took Mrs White's hand and patted it. She seemed surprised. Good. You should always keep a suspect guessing.

"Mya, I'm glad you understand my point of view. Andrew just doesn't get how serious this all is."

"You can cry if you want," I said. "I'll get some tissues. My mum gave me loads, just in case."

"I've already cried a little," she said.

"There is so much to sort out. Where do I start? My work? Our savings? Our house? Our cars? It's overwhelming sometimes!"

She bit her lip and thought for a while. There were tears in her eyes. Slowly she took her hand away from mine.

"Anyway, children shouldn't worry about such things. That's our job as parents."

"But—"

"We'll make this work. Somehow."

"But—"

"You're so sweet. Coming here to check on me like this." She hugged me. "There is absolutely *nothing* to worry about. We can still pay the bills."

Her saying there was nothing to worry about made me worry even more.

"Mya, everything will be sorted out very soon," she said. "I'm just fine, okay?"

"But—"

She ruffled my hair and pinched my cheek.

"Go to sleep, darling," she said happily. "A police officer needs her rest."

She closed the door in my face.

Wait a minute, I thought. How did she know I was a police officer? I hadn't shown her my badge!

A phone rang downstairs. Someone answered it right away.

I tiptoed downstairs and peeked into the living room. Standing by the TV was Mr White. He was on the phone to someone. Who calls someone so early in the morning? Someone who's hiding something! No wonder he talked very quietly.

"Told you," he snapped. "She asked me some questions too!"

He was talking to Mrs White! That's why she took so long to open the door. She wasn't pretending to sleep, she was on the phone to him. He warned her that I was coming!

"I told her *nothing* about us," he cried. "Why would I? It's none of her business."

But it WAS my business! My job is to help British citizens. All of them. Even mean ones like Angel.

"Stay quiet and don't say any more," he said. "Angel doesn't have to know until I get a new job. Then we can break the news to her…"

I'd seen enough.

I tiptoed upstairs and slipped into bed. Angel was pacing up and down, muttering to herself. She stopped and glared at me before turning away.

"I knew I was right," she snapped. "They're divorcing, aren't they? Is that what my mum said?"

Because Mrs White had whispered to me,

Angel hadn't heard that her parents were already divorced.

"Say something, Mya!" she hissed. "Remember what I'm paying you for. Stop their divorce!"

"You wanted to know if they're divorcing. What if I can't stop it?"

"If you don't stop the divorce…" She took out her brand-new mobile phone. "I'll call your boss and take away your badge, got it?"

"But—"

"You'd better stop that divorce!"

How could I stop a divorce that had already happened?

"Did my mum say something or not?" Angel asked, moving closer to the bed. She gripped the mobile so tightly her knuckles turned paper white. "Tell me!"

I couldn't tell her the truth. She would only pay me ten thousand pounds if I stopped the divorce. It was too late. It'd already happened.

"Tell me, Mya!"

If I told the truth, my boss would take away my badge. I'd never be able to solve cases again.

"Say something, Mya!"

I pulled the covers over my head, but she ripped them off and tossed them onto the floor. Then she stood over me, glaring through big, angry eyes.

"What did my mum say to you?" she asked, tapping her foot. "Answer me!"

If I kept the divorce a secret, I could get her parents back together! She would never know the truth.

"Your mum said that…she wants to have dinner with your dad. A date. Just like old times."

"That's a good idea!" Angel clapped.

"That'll stop the divorce because they'll fall in love again."

I hoped she was right. Maybe a date would help them kiss and make up. No arguing or fussing. They'd be holding hands all night.

"A date in the dining room," I said. "Easy peasy. Can you cook?"

"Of course," she snapped. "I can cook cold cereal and warm cereal. Mum said my cereal is the best she's ever tasted!"

Oh boy…

At the time, I thought cooking cereal for dinner would be the hard part. We didn't have wine or anything fancy for them to drink, so milk and water would have to do.

While Angel picked out a pretty dress to wear later, I lay there wondering which cereal we'd add to the menu.

I thought the date would end with Mr and Mrs White holding hands in the moonlight.

Instead, it would end with me hanging upside down, and Angel at the bottom of the swimming pool…

Chapter 10

My plan was simple. We'd get Angel's parents to have dinner together so they'd kiss and make up. Angel would think they weren't divorcing and pay me ten thousand pounds. She wouldn't know they'd already divorced until they got married again.

Easy peasy, I thought. Angel gets what she wants. I get what I want. Everyone gets what they want.

That evening, Angel and I collected all the cereal boxes in the kitchen. Her dad watched us from the living room.

"What're you girls up to?" he asked.

"Nothing, Daddy!" Angel batted her blue eyes. "I love you!"

"Aw, I love you too!"

He turned back to the TV and turned up the volume.

We took the cereal into the dining room and placed the boxes neatly on the table. Angel found some placemats while I got two big bowls and spoons from the kitchen.

"It's got to be…" I thought for a moment. "Romantic!"

"Yes, romantic!" Angel reached into a cupboard and pulled out some candles. "We can't light them. I'm not allowed to use matches."

"Me neither," I said. "Leave the candles on the table so your dad can light them."

Angel dimmed the ceiling lights while I opened the curtains. There was a beautiful view of the back garden. The swimming pool lights made the water twinkle like stars. I hoped it was romantic enough to make her parents fall in love again.

The front door slammed shut and Mrs White called us. We rushed out and Angel gave her mum a big hug.

"What're you ladies doing in there?" Mrs White asked.

"Mummy, can you go upstairs and make yourself look prettier? You and Daddy have a date!"

Mr White came into the hallway. He didn't look very happy about the date.

"Angel, princess, your mother has a lot of work to do."

"Daddy is right, sweetie pie." Her mum kissed her cheeks. "I have to prepare for work tomorrow."

Angel threw herself to the floor and

sobbed. Then she thumped her fists and released a scream so loud my ears hurt.

"All right, darling," her mum said quickly. "Daddy and I will have this date. Just let me take off my suit first."

Angel's mum marched upstairs, muttering under her breath. Mr White stormed back into the living room and fiddled with the video recorder. Seconds later, he was recording the movie on TV.

"What now?" Angel asked.

"We must keep an eye on them," I said. "Make sure they're being romantic instead of arguing."

"But we can't be in the room," she said. "It won't be romantic if we stand there watching them."

"I've got an idea," I said. "Wait here."

I rushed upstairs and found my walkie talkies. Good thing I'd decided to bring them with me. I always brought my police stuff to sleepovers because there might be a case to solve.

I took the walkie talkies downstairs and Angel hid one under the table. I wrapped my hairband around it so the On button stayed pushed in. Now we could hear her parents talking without being in the room.

"We need a back-up plan too," I said. "Just in case something goes wrong."

I remembered Angel throwing her old phone out the window. How did she get a new mobile so quickly? Her mum couldn't buy it because she was at work all day. Her dad didn't buy it because he was at home all day. Her dog didn't buy it because he didn't have any money.

"How did you get a new phone so quickly?" I asked.

"I have five phones," she said.

My eyes popped out my head.

"Why do you have so many?"

"Because the shop sells a new mobile every year. I can't have an old phone like poor people…poor people like *you*."

I rolled my eyes.

"Daddy will buy me a new phone this weekend. I'll use this one for now."

"Have you got your other old phones?"

"Yep."

"Good," I said. "Do they have video chat?"

"Probably, why?"

Earlier that day, I'd talked to my parents on my mobile phone. We'd used the video chat app. It meant I could see them and my gran.

If we used the video chat with Angel's phones, we could leave one phone in the dining room and keep one with us. Then we could watch her parents without them knowing.

I told Angel my plan.

"We're using the walkie talkies *and* the mobiles?" Angel asked. "Good. If one doesn't work properly, the other one will."

"Using video chat means we'll hear AND see your parents," I said. "Let's get the phones ready."

I hid one phone on the fireplace, right behind a family photo. Now we could watch the whole date from upstairs.

"I'm ready for the date," Angel's mum yelled downstairs. "Am I too early?"

I couldn't wait to see what Angel's mum had on. I expected a pretty dress and make-up. Maybe some sparkly earrings with a matching necklace.

Angel and I went into the hallway and looked upstairs. Our mouths gaped open when we saw Mrs White.

"Mrs White, you look so…so…um…"

Angel's mum stood on the top step in dark red pyjamas and fluffy slippers. Her hair was messy, her make-up was smudged and she had a work folder under her arm.

"Mum!" Angel cried. "Where's that pretty dress you wore to Auntie Mary's wedding?"

"That's my best dress, darling. It is locked away for special occasions."

"But isn't *this* special?" Angel asked.

"Of course it is but…"

Mr White came out of the living room. He was in a stained t-shirt and scruffy shorts. He nodded at Mrs White before dragging his feet into the dining room.

Once Angel's parents were at the table, I poured them a glass of water each and left a jug of milk.

Angel poured them cereal and handed

them each a spoon. They tucked into their meals, groaning with delight.

"This porridge is magnificent!" Mr White cried. "The milk is so…milky. The porridge has that…porridge texture. And this spoon is so…spoony."

"I agree," Mrs White said. "The water is perfectly chilled. The unlit candles look stunning. The chair is so comfortable. Girls, you did a fantastic job!"

"It was *my* idea," Angel said quickly. "I planned everything. Mya helped, I guess."

I couldn't believe her! How cheeky!

But I didn't complain or argue. I just kept thinking of the ten thousand pounds and medicine for my gran.

"What's for dessert?" Mr White asked.

"Nothing," Angel said. "Mya didn't get dessert ready."

I bit my lip to stop myself from saying

something very naughty to Angel. We hadn't talked about dessert because we'd forgotten it. That wasn't MY fault. It was OUR fault.

"Never mind," Mr White said. "Girls, go and play. I'll come and read you a story in half an hour."

"Remember to brush your teeth, wash your face, and change into your nighties," Mrs White said, pouring herself more porridge. "Thanks for this date. We haven't had one in such a long time."

Angel and I ran upstairs and climbed under the bedcovers. We held the mobile between us and watched the date using video chat.

"She knows something is wrong," Mrs White whispered. "Angel is not a silly girl."

"She's my daughter too, remember? I know her very well." Mr White pushed the bowl of porridge away. "Bon, is that how you dress on a date? You almost made her cry!"

"What about you?" Mrs White snapped. "Did you even take a shower today?"

"Of course I did…"

"Doesn't smell like it."

"Look, I'm trying here!"

"And I'm not? Just because you don't have a—"

The video chat cut off and back on. Now Mrs White was standing by the door. Mr White was looking out to the garden.

"Angel doesn't need such a big house anyway," Mr White said. "Two smaller ones would be just fine."

"Two?" Mrs White laughed. "Why two?"

"You want us to live in one? But what about—"

The video chat cut off again. When it turned back on, her parents were both by the back window.

"I can't imagine us living in two different homes," Mr White said sadly. "You in one place and me in another."

"Well, it's *your* fault! How could you do this to our family? Why didn't you tell me that you wanted—"

The video chat cut off again.

We waited for it to turn back on.

We waited. And waited. And waited.

Something was wrong with the phone downstairs. It'd worked just fine when I left it on the fireplace.

"Um, Angel, why's it gone off?"

"It's my very old phone," she said. "I haven't used it in two years."

"Okay, so why's the video chat gone off?"

"Well…I forgot to charge the battery."

"So the phone's just died?"

She nodded, her cheeks turning bright pink.

"We can still use the walkie talkie," I said. "Just keep your voice down so they don't hear us, okay?"

I turned on the walkie talkie and held it between us. At first, I couldn't hear anything, but the red light showed it was definitely on.

"Is it working?" Angel asked.

"Quiet!" I whispered. "They'll hear you!"

Too late.

"What was that noise?" Mr White asked. His heavy footsteps stomped across the dining room. "It came from under the table."

Angel and I grabbed each other by the hand and squeezed. We closed our eyes and didn't say a word. I was even scared to breathe, just in case Mr White heard that too.

"I can see a red light under the table," Mr White said. "What is that?"

He must've been looking at the walkie talkie we'd hidden.

"Bonnie, look!" Mr White said. "I think that's a…"

Please don't see the walkie talkie, I thought. Please don't see it! Please don't see it! Please don't see it…

Chapter 11

Mr White was about to find the walkie talkie. If he turned it off, Angel and I couldn't hear the date anymore.

"Andrew, stop changing the subject!" Mrs White snapped. "It's probably one of the girls' toys."

Angel and I sighed with relief.

"Bonnie, we have to accept that our old lives are over. From now on, things will be different."

"I know that," Mrs White said.

It went quiet for a bit.

"Bonnie, I've got some paperwork you need to sign. Then we can move ahead with things."

Angel covered the walkie talkie with her hands and gently placed it down. We moved outside to the balcony where no one could hear us.

"See? I was right! They're divorcing!"

"What? Because your mum is signing paperwork? My dad signs papers for work. It's no big deal!"

"This is different," she said. "When my friend's parents broke up, they signed papers. *Divorce* papers!"

Why would Angel's parents sign divorce papers if they'd already divorced?

"We need to see those papers," I said. "They might be divorce papers. They might not be…"

Angel leaned in until our noses touched.

Her pointy nose poked my round one, making it hurt.

"Do you think they're divorcing or not?" she asked.

"…Yes."

I couldn't tell her they'd already divorced. If she found out, she'd get angry and tell my boss to fire me!

"I want to see those papers," she spat. "I want to see them right now!"

How could we see the papers without her parents knowing? I had an idea…

"We're going into the garden," I said. "We'll look through the back window and see inside the dining room."

We crept downstairs and stopped by the back door. There was a tiny box on the wall with numbers on it. It looked like the burglar alarm we had at home.

"Don't tell anyone the code!" Angel spat.

"It's a secret!"

She pressed some numbers and the box bleeped twice. Then she slid open the back door and we tiptoed outside.

"Stay down and stay quiet," I whispered.

We sneaked across the garden and stopped by the dining room window.

I turned the walkie talkie volume down really low and held it against my ear.

"Is that the paperwork?" Mrs White asked. I could hear some papers rustling. "That's a lot to sign."

"Once it's signed, it'll be a fresh start for us."

Angel peered through the window and squinted. She pressed her face against the glass and shook her head.

"I can't read the papers like this," she whispered. "Wait here!"

She crept across the garden and went into

the shed. She brought back a pair of sparkly, pink binoculars.

Using the binoculars, she looked through the window and watched in silence. I kept listening through the walkie talkie.

"Sign here and here and here," Mr White said. "Oh, and here too."

"Those are the divorce papers," Angel whispered. "I can't let her sign them!"

You're too late, I thought. They're already divorced.

"I want them to love each other again," Angel said. "I want my old family back."

Now I felt guilty. I should've told her they'd already divorced. It'd make her so angry, but at least she'd know the truth.

A good police officer is honest, I thought. Lying is wrong. I shouldn't have done it.

When she found out the truth, she wouldn't pay me ten thousand pounds.

Instead, she'd have me kicked off the Children's Police Force.

"Angel, there's something I have to tell you…"

"Tell me later," she snapped. "Mum's almost done signing the papers. I've got to stop her!"

Angel ran into the house and pressed more numbers on the burglar alarm. It bleeped louder and louder and louder.

Uh oh, I thought. This doesn't look good…

Suddenly the alarm came on. The noise was so loud it hurt my ears. Angel tried turning it off, but she kept pressing the wrong buttons. Every time she entered the wrong code, the alarm got louder.

"My parents are coming!"

"I know," I said. "We've got to hide!"

"Let's go outside," she said. "We can hide

in the shed!"

We dashed across the garden and slipped into the shed. Angel stayed at the back by the lawnmower. I kept the door open a little, watching the garden.

Angel's parents ran outside. Her mum had an umbrella in her hand. Her dad had two tennis rackets.

"Who's there?" Mr White yelled. "We don't want any trouble. Just leave!"

"Drew, this is a bad idea," Mrs White said. "Let's just grab the girls and go in the basement."

"And let a bunch of kids steal our stuff?" Mr White cried. "Not a chance!"

"Okay, okay, but if things go wrong, we're calling the police."

"Fine by me."

The police? I thought. If they come, we'll be in even bigger trouble...

"What're we going to do?" Angel asked.

"You should've thought of that before!" I said. "Why did you do that?"

"I don't want them signing divorce papers. I want them to stay married forever."

Angel sat on the lawnmower and buried her face in her hands.

"You don't understand, Mya. Your parents are happy. Mine are sad."

"We can make them happy again," I said. "We just have to stop the divorce."

When I turned back, Mr White was heading straight for the shed. Mrs White followed him, swinging the umbrella like a sword.

"They're coming," I whispered. "Is there anywhere to hide in here?"

"No," Angel whispered back.

She was right. The shed had six garden chairs, a folded table, a lawnmower, a shovel, a bucket, and a box full of pink toys. There was nowhere to hide.

But then I looked up and saw a tiny window. Angel's eyes followed mine. We just had to get up there.

We unfolded the table and climbed on top. Angel pushed me out of the way and grabbed the window ledge. She managed to pull herself up. Then she slid out the window and landed by a rosebush.

"I heard movement in the shed," Mr White said.

"Let's go in!"

"On the count of three. One…"

I grabbed the window and pulled myself up. It was very hard. I kept wriggling until I was halfway out.

"Two…"

Angel reached up and pulled my hands. She tugged and tugged, but my trouser pocket was caught on the window frame. I ripped my trousers free, leaving a big hole in the pocket.

"Three!" Mr White shouted. "Time's up! Ready or not, here we come…"

Chapter 12

I fell out the window and landed face first in a rosebush. The thorns caught onto my afro hair and tugged. It hurt a lot, so I rubbed my aching head.

"Let's go back to my bedroom," Angel whispered. "Hurry up!"

We crawled through the bushes, peeking out to see where her parents were. They were still searching for burglars in the shed.

Soon Angel and I reached the other end of the garden. Now all we had to do was get back inside.

"Are you ready?" Angel whispered.

I nodded.

"One…two…three…go!"

I rushed ahead, keeping my eyes on the back door. Soon we'd be in bed upstairs. Hopefully we had time to get changed into our pyjamas before Mr White came to read us a story.

When I looked back, Angel ran too close to the swimming pool. I knew that was bad. It's dangerous to run next to a pool because the floor is slippery. You might fall and bang your head.

Luckily Angel didn't bang her head, but she did fall. She toppled over and landed on the grass. Her shoes kept slipping in mud when she tried to stand up.

"Is someone out there?" Mrs White yelled. "Drew, get ready!"

Her parents were coming out soon. We

had to hurry!

"Come on," I whispered. "They'll catch us!"

"I can't…get up…Mya!"

My trainers easily gripped the grass, but Angel's pretty shoes kept slipping. If she didn't get up soon, we'd be caught by her parents.

"Do something!" Angel hissed.

I took a quick look around and saw a light switch by the door. I flipped it and the swimming pool lights cut out.

Now the garden was so dark I could barely see. I crept over to Angel, being very careful not to fall in the pool.

"The burglars put the lights out," Mrs White said. "Andrew, do something!"

"Can't you see that I'm trying?"

"I can't see anything!"

Angel and I huddled by the pool. She was

shaking. I was scared too.

"They'll turn the lights back on soon," Angel whispered. "We have to hide again."

The bushes were a great place to hide, but they were too far away. We wouldn't get there before the lights came back on.

We couldn't run to the house because her parents were heading that way. I could hear them trudging through the grass.

We also couldn't stay by the swimming pool. When the pool lights came on, her parents would easily see us.

I looked up and squinted. My eyes got used to the darkness. Now I could see the diving board. It was close by.

"We can hide up there," I whispered.

We climbed the ladder to the diving board. If we got high enough, Angel's parents wouldn't see us when the lights came on.

At the top, Angel and I lay flat on the

diving board. It was much higher than it looked from the ground. The garden and pool looked so far down.

"Turn the lights on!" Mrs White cried.

The pool lights came on. We were so high up it was still dark on the diving board.

"Check the bushes," Mrs White said. "I'll call the police."

Uh oh…I couldn't let her call the police! You should only call them in an emergency. This wasn't an emergency!

"We have to go down," I said. "I can't let your mum call the police. They're very busy helping people."

Angel grabbed my wrist and held on so tightly it hurt. I tried to wriggle free but she was too strong.

"Mya, we're NOT going down there!"

"Why not?"

"Because we'll be in BIG trouble," she

hissed.

"Just cry like you did earlier," I said. "That always seems to work."

"Crying won't work this time."

"Why not? It made your parents go on the date, even though they didn't want to."

"I can't use cry-baby tears twice in one day. It doesn't work after the first time." She squeezed my wrist even tighter. "Without cry-baby tears, we'll be in big trouble if we're caught. Just stay up here until they go back inside."

"But your mum is *scared*," I said. "She thinks we're burglars."

"So what?"

"The police will come and see there's no burglars here. Your parents might be told off for wasting the police's time!"

"I don't care," she hissed. "You're *not* going down there. Just keep still. They'll go inside soon."

Mrs White took out the mobile phone from her pyjama pocket. She kept her eyes on Mr White, who was checking the rosebushes.

"Angel, let go of me!"

"No!"

She squeezed my arm tighter.

"It's wrong to call the police when you don't need them," I said. "I've got to stop her!"

"No!"

I tugged my arm but she held on. I tugged again, so she squeezed tighter. Now my arm was very sore.

"It hurts," I whispered. "Let go!"

"No!"

I stopped for a moment to gather all my strength. Then after a very deep breath, I tore my arm away from her.

Unfortunately, I did it a bit too hard.

Angel fell backwards and rolled over the diving board. I threw myself forward and grabbed her leg, but it slid down my hand. Soon I was holding on to her ankle while she dangled upside down.

"Hello?" Mrs White said. "I think we have burglars!"

Angel was too heavy to hold. I found myself slipping over the edge of the diving board. Seconds later, half my body was over the side.

"Pull me up," Angel whispered. "And be quick!"

Her parents rushed back into the house, still holding the umbrella and tennis rackets.

"I think the burglars just spoke to each other," Mrs White said. "They might be planning something. Please hurry!"

Letting Mrs White call the police for no reason wasn't good. It was bad. Very bad. But

I couldn't stop her if I was busy holding on to Angel's leg.

When I looked down at Angel, she gave me the meanest look ever.

"Don't you *dare* drop me in that water," she spat. "This is my favourite dress! And I spent five whole minutes brushing my hair this morning."

She kept talking but I stopped listening. We both knew she wouldn't change my mind. I'd already decided what to do next.

A good police officer always does the right thing, I thought. Even if it gets them into trouble.

So, I let go…

Chapter 13

Everything happened so fast.

I yelled for Mrs White to put down the phone. She jumped from fright, and then jumped again when Angel hit the water. Mr White dived in and pulled Angel out. When she felt her soggy curls and saw her soaked dress, she starting screaming at me.

"Sorry, officer, we don't need assistance after all," Mrs White said. She shoved the mobile into her pyjama pocket and glared at Angel. "Drew, get her toys."

"But, Mummy—"

"I wasn't talking to *you*, young lady!"

Mr White grabbed Angel's toys and dumped them in a cardboard box. He took the box out to the shed and locked it away.

Mrs White marched Angel and I upstairs to the bathroom. I washed the grass, twigs and mud off me. Angel was cleaner because she'd been in the pool, so she just washed off chlorine. Then we went straight to bed.

"It's not time to sleep yet," Mrs White said. "We need to talk."

Mrs White gave me an angry look from time to time, but only yelled at Angel.

"What on earth were you thinking?" Mrs White cried. "Angel, answer me!"

Angel started crying.

"Those crocodile tears will not work this time," her mum snapped. "I asked a question. Answer it!"

"We wanted to—"

"You should know better, young lady!" Her mum started pacing up and down the bedroom. "You're several months older than Mya. You are supposed to set a good example to younger children."

"She dropped me in the pool!" Angel cried.

"Good," her mum said. "You shouldn't have been up there in the first place!"

"But—"

"When my mouth is open, yours should be shut," her mum said.

Angel shut her mouth and kept it shut.

Mrs White lectured us for an hour. First, she told us off for scaring her and Mr White. Next, she told us off for playing by the pool without supervision. Finally, she told us off for touching the burglar alarm.

"We will continue this talk tomorrow morning," she said. "I'm too busy right now.

I have a big work project and little time to prepare."

"Sorry, Mummy."

"Do you know what hurts most?" Mrs White asked. "I thought the dinner date was a treat for your father and me. Instead it was a distraction so you could run around unattended."

"That's not why—"

"Goodnight, ladies." Mrs White kissed us both on the head. "I have an important call to make."

A call? In the late evening? Who was she calling?

When Mrs White stormed out, Angel and I slipped under the covers. We lay in silence, back to back. I didn't want to see her right now. She didn't want to see me either.

"This was all your dumb idea," Angel said. "What kind of police officer are you?"

"A good one," I said. "I didn't let your mum call the police for no reason. She would've been in trouble!"

"Well now YOU are in trouble…"

"What's *that* supposed to mean?"

"Who'd you think she's calling?"

I had no idea.

"Mum might be calling the office," she said. "She did say she's got lots of work. She would've finished her work already if you didn't set up that stupid date!"

I couldn't believe she was blaming everything on me!

"Or Mum might be calling the burglar alarm company. If we don't call them, they might send the police to our house."

That would be pretty bad. I didn't want to waste the police's time. They were busy solving lots of big cases.

"Or Mum might be calling…" She

giggled.

"Calling who?"

"Mum might be calling…*your* mum!"

I jumped out of bed and ran into the hallway. I could hear Angel's parents arguing downstairs. Then Mrs White stormed into the living room and slammed the door shut.

I crept downstairs and pressed my ear against the living room door. Luckily Mr White stayed in the kitchen or I would've been in even more trouble.

"Hello?" Mrs White said. "Hello, this is Bonnie, Angel's mum. Could I speak to Mrs Dove, please?"

My whole body was shaking now. Dad telling me off was bad, but Mum telling me off was much worse.

"Hello, Rose, how is your mother-in-law? That's great news!" It was quiet for a bit. "Mya? Well, that's what I'm calling about…"

Heavy footsteps were coming from the kitchen. Prince came out first and started growling at me.

"What's wrong?" Mr White asked, sounding close by. He'd catch me any second now!

I rushed upstairs to Angel's bedroom. Huffing and puffing away, I slipped into bed and pulled the covers over my head. Angel kept her back to me, giggling away.

"Told you," she said. "She's calling your mum, isn't she?"

Yes, she was.

My mobile was on the bedside table. I watched it closely. Soon the phone would vibrate and start ringing. It would be my mum and dad, and they'd be furious...

Chapter 14

I didn't sleep very well. Every time my phone buzzed, I thought it was my parents calling to tell me off. Instead, it was just my brother sending photos of him partying with friends. It wasn't fair! He was having so much fun while I was stuck with Angel.

When my alarm went off, I had to drag myself out of bed. My body was still very tired and sore from the night before.

"Did you sleep all right?" Angel asked, grinning. "No? Good!"

She skipped downstairs while I dragged

my feet behind her. My mobile was in my pyjama pocket. I could've left it in the bedroom, but what if I missed Mum's call? That would make her even more mad!

When we got downstairs, the kitchen was completely silent. Angel's parents were waiting at the table for us. Mr White had bags under his eyes. Mrs White was red-faced, just like the day before.

It was a tough breakfast. No TV. No phones allowed. No newspapers either. Just the four of us eating breakfast in our dressing gowns. Her parents only spoke to us when they had to.

"Good morning," they said.

"Good morning," we said.

"What would you like for breakfast?" Mrs White asked.

"Cereal, please," we said.

"What would you like to drink?" Mr

White asked.

"Orange juice, please," we said.

Angel's parents were very quiet after that.

"Mummy, are you okay?" Angel asked.

Mrs White kept sipping her coffee. She didn't even look Angel's way.

"Daddy, how's your sausages?" Angel asked, batting her blue eyes.

Her dad creased his brow and kept chewing his sausages and eggs. He didn't look at Angel either.

Suddenly Mrs White stood up and took her cup to the sink. She washed it quickly before leaving the kitchen. Seconds later, she was stomping around upstairs.

"You girls had us very worried," Mr White whispered. "We thought there was a burglar out there!"

"Yay, you're talking to me again!" Angel rushed over to hug her dad. "I love you,

Daddy!"

"I love you too, but the point is…" He stopped to hug her. Then he reached across the table and ruffled my afro puff. "You girls were supposed to be in bed. Why were you outside?"

"Mr White, we were—"

"Going on a bear hunt," Angel said quickly.

"A bear hunt?" her dad asked, looking confused. "In the garden?"

"Yeah, but not for *real* bears, duh!" She pretended to laugh. "A real bear wouldn't live in our garden. Bears need more space."

"So you girls were on a bear hunt, eh?" Mr White narrowed his eyes. "Tell me, Officer Mya, why was there a walkie talkie in the dining room?"

Lots of possible reasons rushed through my mind. Some were good and some were bad.

"Mr White, the bear could've gone through the window into the dining room. Then it might've run around the house."

"A bear in the house…That reminds me of Goldilocks and the Three Bears," he said. "Goldilocks sat in the bears' chairs, ate their food and then slept in their beds. It was rude to do that without permission!"

"Calm down, Daddy," Angel said, patting him on the head. "It's not a true story."

Angel was right. There's no way Goldilocks could really do all that. She couldn't sneak into a bear's house because bears live in caves, not houses. She couldn't eat their porridge because bears eat veg and fish.

I wasn't sure if bears had chairs. I was too scared to go into a cave and find out!

"Mr White, we didn't want bears coming

into the house, sitting in our chairs, eating our porridge and sleeping in our beds! That's why we went on a bear hunt."

I hoped he believed us. The whole bear hunt story sounded so silly. Couldn't Angel think of a better lie than that? I hadn't been on a bear hunt since I was five!

"I understand," Mr White said. "I don't want a bear in my bed. There wouldn't be enough space for Mrs White and I to sleep."

Mrs White walked in. Her dressing gown was gone now. She'd changed into a dark grey trouser suit with short high heels.

Her cheeks were pink and her face was sweaty. She had a massive suitcase behind her and a wash bag in her hand.

"All that for one night?" Mr White asked. "You sure you aren't moving out?"

They both laughed. Angel didn't find it funny. Neither did I.

"I'm taking extra work with me," Mrs White said, patting the suitcase. "It's so boring in that hotel."

I reached into my pocket and pulled out the divorce signs article Angel had printed. One of the signs was a parent working away from home a lot.

Angel saw what I was reading and gulped, her face going pale.

"Does your mum work away from home a lot?" I whispered.

"She never did before, but now she does. Maybe because she doesn't love my dad anymore."

Mrs White checked the clock on the wall and threw her hands up. In a huff, she pulled on her coat and wrapped a scarf around her neck.

"I didn't know you'd be leaving so soon," Mr White said sadly. "I thought we had more time."

"I have to do this." She tidied her blonde wig. "How do I look?"

"Beautiful," Mr White said.

Mrs White blushed.

Why's he being so nice to her? I wondered. They're divorced now. They don't love each other anymore.

"Drew, remember to—"

"Feed the girls and the dog," Mr White said. "I know, I know."

"Call Mya's parents to—"

"Remind them that you'll be away." Mr White yawned. "I know, I know."

"Remind them?" I asked.

"Yes, I called your mother yesterday evening," Mrs White said. "I told her I'd be away from home. She'll call Mr White if she needs to get in touch, okay?"

"Oh, I thought…"

"No, Mya, I didn't tell her about last night," Mrs White said.

Angel frowned and crossed her arms, muttering under her breath.

"Thanks for not telling on me," I said.

"They have enough on their plate with your grandmother being ill…but she's feeling much better, which is great news!"

Mrs White's phone buzzed. She glanced at the screen and smiled.

"Well, I'm off!"

Mrs White hugged Angel and I, kissed Mr White on the cheek and rushed out the front door.

Prince's ears flopped down and he shuffled to his bed. Mrs White had forgotten to tell him goodbye.

"Mr White, where's she going?"

"To Germany. Her clients need to see her about a very important project." He put a finger to his lips. "It's top secret!"

"Like my police cases."

"Exactly."

Mr White glanced at the front door and sighed.

"What's wrong, Daddy?"

"I've always wanted to travel like that…I'm a little jealous. Then again, she's probably envious of me too. She's off early in the morning while I relax at home."

"I thought you had work too," I said.

Mr White's face turned very pale.

"Yes, I have work too. Nothing to worry about."

"Is something wrong with your job?" I asked.

"Nope. Everything is fine. I'm just taking a break before I start some new projects."

His phone rang. He rushed to the kitchen counter to answer it.

"Good morning…Yes, this is Mr White speaking. Caroline Robbins? Oh, Caroline! It's great to hear from you about…" He lowered his voice. "The job opportunity. In Switzerland. Yes, I have always wanted to visit the country. What a beautiful place."

Switzerland? That was somewhere in Europe. A different country? Was Mr White moving THAT far away?

Now Angel had tears in her eyes. With her head down, she walked off to the back door and stood outside in the garden. Prince went after her and rested his head on her fluffy slippers.

"I'll fly out for an interview," Mr White said. "Yes, I'm available to start immediately."

How could he start a new job right away? What about his old one?

His job is very strange, I thought. He

sleeps in late, stays at home all day, doesn't seem to do any work…

Angel came over and grabbed me by the arm. She pulled me upstairs and only let go to slam her bedroom door behind us.

"I want those divorce papers!" Angel spat. "And I want them right now!"

"Well, I don't have them."

"I know that, Mya, but you have to find them." She took out her mobile phone and dangled it in my face. "Or I'll call your boss and get you fired."

"You can't do that to me!"

"No more cases for you," she said. "No more badge. No more handcuffs. No more walkie talkies. No more grapes!"

No more grapes? That made me cry. She didn't even offer a tissue. Instead, she tossed her phone onto the bed and started getting changed.

"Aren't you gonna wash?" I asked, still sniffling.

"Get changed. Just spray my perfume over your body."

"That's gross!"

She pulled on sparkly shoes and a pretty pink dress. Then she threw open my suitcase and rummaged through my clothes, tossing out trousers, a t-shirt and a headband.

"Where are we going?" I asked.

"To the garage."

"What's in there?" I asked, my throat tightening.

"Lots of things," she replied. "We keep our cars outside. No one keeps cars in the garage anymore."

"We don't need to go in there, do we?"

"Yes, we do."

I remembered their three, dusty spare rooms. I didn't mind dust or dirt, but there was something I DID mind…

"Is the garage clean and tidy?" I asked.

"Why? Do you have dust allergies or something?" She had a confused look on her face. "We must get to the garage before Daddy leaves for Switzerland. We have to find it before he hides it!"

"Hides what?"

"The divorce papers!" she cried. "They must be hidden in the garage…or the basement."

I couldn't go in the basement! What if THEY were down there? They were big, hairy and very scary! Their cobwebs were probably HUGE down there. Big enough to catch me in them! Angel wouldn't help me. I'd be stuck down there forever.

"Fine, let's go to the garage!" I said quickly.

If I got stuck in a giant cobweb in the

garage, I could scream really loud until Mr White heard me. He might not hear me screaming in the basement.

A loud rumbling noise came from outside. We rushed to the balcony and looked down below.

Still in his dressing gown, Mr White was standing by the garage door. It opened slowly. He kept looking over his shoulder as if someone might be watching.

"I told you," Angel whispered. "See? He's going in there to get rid of the divorce papers!"

"Then we're too late," I said.

I knew they were already divorced, but Angel didn't know that…yet.

"Mya, if you don't stop him…" She glanced over at her mobile. Soon she'd call my boss. I thought of my badge being taken away. "Mya, get down there. Now!"

I dashed out and rushed downstairs. I threw open the front door and sprinted to the garage.

When I ran inside, my feet froze to the spot. My eyes couldn't believe what they were seeing.

"Oh, Mya," Mr White said. "I wish you hadn't seen this…"

Chapter 15

"Seen what?" Angel cried, running up behind me. Her jaw dropped when she saw the garage. "Whoa…"

Inside were two treadmills, an exercise bike, a rowing machine, a workout step, and stretchy fitness bands my mum used to exercise.

"Your mother and I watched far too many fitness infomercials. We bought almost *everything* they sold." He laughed nervously. "We can't spend like that anymore…"

"We can, Daddy! We're rich, not poor like

Mya."

"I'm not poor," I snapped. "I'm just not rich."

"There is nothing wrong with being low or middle class," Mr White said. "Not everyone earns as much as we used to…as much as we do now."

Angel pushed past me to hug her dad. While they hugged, her narrow eyes scanned the garage.

"Daddy," she said softly, "what are you looking for?"

"Just a book on German," he said. "I need to brush up on my skills before I travel to Switzerland. I haven't spoken German in so long."

"But what about your job?" I asked. "You can't just leave, can you?"

Mr White turned away and searched through some boxes. I wanted to go into the garage and ask him about work again, but I couldn't. There was a massive spiderweb near the door. I didn't want that thing to touch me!

"There it is!" Mr White pulled out a book with *Learn to Speak German* on the cover in big letters. "Let's go back inside, shall we?"

"Not yet," Angel said. "I need to find something too."

"What, darling princess?"

"A toy."

Mr White took a quick look around and shrugged.

"I can't see many toys about," he said. "Are you sure you left it in here?"

"Yep, a very long time ago. I borrowed it from Mya when we were best friends."

"We weren't BEST friends," I muttered.

We *were* best friends, but I didn't want anyone to know that. She was a mean girl now. She wasn't back then.

"Have you checked the guest rooms?" Mr White asked. "They are packed with toys."

"It's in the garage, I know it!" Angel let go of him and started looking through boxes. "Mya, help me look!"

"I can't…"

A big spider was staring at me. Every time I took a step closer to Angel, the spider twitched.

I wish this garage was clean like ours, I thought. Mum always dusts the ceiling and walls. There's no spiders in our house. Mum puts them all outside.

"I'll leave you both to it," Mr White said. "I need to practise my German. It's been so long…"

He strolled back into the house and closed the front door.

Angel kept searching through each

cardboard box. She tore open the top, threw everything out, shook her head angrily, and moved on to the next box.

Soon the garage was a mess. I could barely see her behind the massive pile of empty cardboard boxes, old newspapers and magazines, exercise stuff and broken toys.

"I don't think their divorce papers are in there," I said, my eyes still on the evil spider. "Let's go back inside."

I expected Angel to put everything away. Instead, she kicked it all to the side and pushed a button on the wall. The door started to close as she stepped outside.

"I'm going to ask Daddy where the divorce papers are," she said. "Then I'm going to tear them up and put them in the bin!"

Angel stormed back into the house while I begged her to stop. If her dad told her it was too late to stop the divorce, she would be *really* angry. She'd take it all out on me.

"Angel, wait a minute!"

"No more silly police stuff," she snapped. "I'm going to ask him if they're divorcing."

She pushed open the kitchen door, huffed and turned to the stairs.

"Daddy? Where are you?"

There was a loud humming upstairs. It sounded just like my dad's shaver.

"The divorce papers might be in the dining room," I said.

"They wouldn't leave divorce papers just lying around," she said. "When my friend's parents divorced, they kept the divorce papers locked away."

"Then we'll find them!"

"We tried that already and it's taking too long," she said. "It'd be much quicker to ask my parents if they're divorcing."

"They might not tell you!"

"Then at least we tried," she said, pushing me out the way. She stopped at the bottom of the stairs. "Daddy, I want to talk to you right now!"

The humming upstairs stopped. Something heavy dropped on the floor and Angel's dad said a naughty word. Then he stomped down the landing and stopped near the stairs. I couldn't see him from where I was standing.

"Um…" Angel's eyes widened. "Um, Daddy, we need to talk."

"In five minutes."

He stomped off and closed a door upstairs.

"What's wrong?" I asked.

"He looks…*different*," she said. "You'll see."

We waited for five minutes. He never came down. We waited another five minutes.

He still didn't show up. Then another five minutes went by.

By now, Angel's face had turned dark red. She was tapping her foot and muttering under her breath. Her angry eyes glared at the clock ticking away in the kitchen.

"Mya," she snapped, "get upstairs now!"

"But—"

Angel grabbed my arm and pulled me behind her. I found myself being dragged upstairs until we reached the top.

"Let's ask Daddy," she said. "Are you ready?"

No! Angel was about to hear that her parents were already divorced. Then she might figure out I already knew. I was wrong to keep it a secret, but it was too late now. She was about to find out the truth.

Halfway down the landing, she stopped and cried, "Daddy, where are you?"

"In the bedroom, why?"

She stopped outside her parents' room and tried to open the door. It was locked.

"Open up!" she cried. "We need to talk!"

"Just a minute, darling princess. Daddy is drying his hair." He turned on the hairdryer. "I won't be long, I promise!"

Several minutes went by, and then several more. Angel didn't like that very much. She thumped her fist on the door over and over again.

"Open up! Open up! Open up!"

I hoped he didn't. When she found out her parents had divorced, she wouldn't pay me ten thousand pounds. I needed that money to buy lots of medicine for Granny. It'd help her get better much faster.

"Open up! Open up! Open up!"

The hairdryer stopped.

The door unlocked.

Angel and I held our breaths.

Nobody moved.

"You coming in?" Mr White asked. "You still there?"

"Wait here," Angel said. "I've got to do this on my own."

Good. I didn't want to be around when her dad told her the truth. I knew she'd start screaming, tearing things, smashing things and throwing things.

Angel opened the door and stepped inside. Then she screamed and ran out…

Chapter 16

Angel screamed and ran from her parents' bedroom. She dashed to her room and hid behind the bed.

"Did you see him?" she cried.

"Nope," I said. "Was he, you know, in his underpants?"

"No, that's gross!" Angel stuck out her tongue. "No, he…"

Heavy footsteps headed our way. Angel's door opened a crack and a blue eye peered inside. I lowered down and didn't move. I didn't know why we were hiding, but I didn't want to find out.

"Princess, let me explain, please."

Angel put a finger to her lips.

The door opened and Mr White walked in. He had his dressing gown hood pulled over his head. He stopped by the playhouse and peeked inside the windows.

"Where could my princess and her lovely friend be?" he asked himself. "Nope. Not in the playhouse."

Then he went out to the balcony and stood, hands on hips, shaking his head.

"Nope, the girls aren't here either. Aha! I know where to look…"

Mr White rushed back inside and jumped onto the bed. He tickled our necks, making us giggle.

"So, ladies, tell me how I look."

It was hard to see his suit under his dressing gown, but I could see his hair was a different colour.

Mr White shook off his dressing gown and stood with his head held high. I looked him up and down.

An hour ago, he was scruffy-looking in his stained dressing gown. His beard was bushy with bits of food stuck in it. For the past week, he'd stayed in his pyjamas until the late afternoon.

But now…

Mr White had on a dark blue suit with matching shiny shoes. In his jacket pocket were a pair of glasses and a light blue handkerchief with the letters "AW" (Andrew White) on it.

And he'd changed even more than his clothes and shoes. His teeth didn't look a bit yellow anymore. Now they were whiter than the paper I wrote my case files on. He stood taller, smiled more, and his eyes twinkled a bit.

The biggest change was his hair. His shaggy blond hair was gone. Now it was dark red and straight.

"I hate it!" Angel squealed. "I don't like *ginger* hair."

"That's enough, young lady," Mr White said, his smile turning upside down. "I needed a change. I have an important job interview coming up soon."

"I don't like it! I don't like it! I don't like it!" Angel stomped her feet over and over again. "I don't like it! I don't like it! I don't like it!"

"Officer Dove, what do you think?"

"I like it," I said. "Red is a nice colour. Blue is my favourite, though."

"I'd love to have blue hair," he said. "Maybe one day…"

Mr White picked up the dressing gown

and strolled back to his bedroom. He hummed a merry tune on the way.

Angel pulled me over to the balcony, tears in her eyes. She pulled the divorce signs article out of my pocket and skimmed over it. She stopped near the bottom and sobbed.

"Red hair isn't bad," I said. "Not everyone wants curly blonde hair like yours."

"Mya, I *love* red hair."

"So why'd you say something so mean?"

"Because…"

Angel pointed at the article. I read it.

"A sign that your parents are divorcing is when they change their appearance. They look better now because they want to marry someone else."

"Do you see now?" Angel wept. "He's been horrible-looking for weeks. Now he's looking nice again. Why? Because he doesn't love my mum anymore."

"You don't know that."

"Mya, he's going to find another mummy and have another baby with her." Angel buried her head in her hands. "Then he won't want me anymore. He'll have another princess. A prettier one. A smarter one. A *nicer* one."

I couldn't believe it. Did Angel just admit that she was mean?

"I know I'm a bit mean sometimes, but that's everyone else's fault."

"I'm not sure about that…"

"If I was nicer, maybe you'd still be my best friend. Maybe my parents wouldn't be splitting up. Maybe my daddy would still love me and my mum."

Angel sat on the floor and closed her eyes. Tears trickled down her cheeks. I wiped them away with my hand and she smiled. It was a warm smile, not the mean ones she usually gave. I hadn't seen her nice smile in a very, very long time.

"You are the best friend I've ever had," she said. "My friends at school do whatever I say. It's so boring when people agree with you all the time."

"I thought you liked when people do what you want."

"I do, but not all the time," she said. "Sometimes I want a friend like you. You do whatever you want. Just like me."

I did miss being her friend. At nursery, we learned our ABCs together, counted to thirty together, and even coloured in pictures together.

Being in nursery was so much fun! Painting, reading picture books, building sandcastles in the sandpit, and playing with dolls in the playhouse. We did all that together.

Until she was mean.

But now she was being nice to me. I wondered if the old Angel was back. Maybe that's why she was being so honest with me.

It was time for me to be honest too.

"Angel," I said, my hands shaking, "I have something to tell you."

"What is it, Mya?" she asked, wiping her puffy red eyes. "Just tell me. I won't be mad, I promise."

"Well, the other day your mum whispered a secret to me. She told me that your parents are already divorced."

Angel stared blankly at me.

"Did you hear me?" I asked, my voice trembling. "Your parents are already divorced."

She didn't move. She didn't blink. I wasn't sure if she was even breathing.

"Angel, we can't stop your parents'

divorce. It's already happened."

Angel's warm smile faded and her mean grin came back. Her blue eyes narrowed as her face moved closer to mine.

"Angel, say something…"

She grabbed me by the shoulders and squeezed so hard it hurt. I wriggled as much as I could but she wouldn't let go.

"Are you saying my parents have already divorced? Are you saying the case is over?" She squeezed harder, her eyes bulging. "Oh, I see what's REALLY going on here…"

Chapter 17

"There's nothing going on," I said to Angel. "Your parents already divorced! It's too late to stop them."

"Liar!" she spat. "I see what you're up to!"

"What're you on about?"

"It's almost the weekend. You'll be going home soon. You don't care about the case anymore."

"I NEVER give up on a case! I always try my best, even when time's running out. Just ask Jimmy and Libby!"

Angel let out a very loud scream. My ears

hurt a lot.

"Angel, stop screaming!" her dad yelled from his bedroom.

"Sorry, Daddy," she said. "Mya's being mean!"

"No, I'm not," I said. "I'm just telling you the truth."

"The truth is you won't solve this case anymore because…because…because you're a *scaredy-cat*!" She stuck out her tongue. "A brave police officer would've searched the garage with me. You weren't brave. You were scared…"

"But there was a spider in there…"

"A brave police officer wouldn't be scared of a tiny spider."

Tiny? I thought. It was HUGE! Maybe even bigger than her dog. Maybe. Maybe not.

"You're wrong about the divorce and I'm going to prove it," she said. "When we find the divorce papers, you'll see they haven't divorced yet."

"No, YOU are wrong," I said. "When we find the divorce papers, you'll see that your parents are already divorced."

"Find the papers and prove it!"

"But we've looked *everywhere!*" I cried.

"Actually, there are three places we haven't looked yet."

"The attic?"

"It's dark, cold and dirty," she said. "Nobody goes up there."

"Where else, then?"

"My mum's car," Angel said. "She left it at the airport, but she'll drive it back tomorrow!"

"What about your dad's car?"

"Mum took it to the garage on Monday morning."

"Okay, so what's the last place we haven't

looked?"

"The basement," she whispered.

For the whole day, all I could think about was the basement. I imagined it was full of dust, damp, junk, and lots of evil spiders.

At bedtime, I found it hard to fall asleep. Every time I closed my eyes, I imagined the massive spiders waiting in the basement.

I didn't sleep very well that night.

The next morning, I got up early and called my mum. I tried to sound happy, but she could tell something was wrong.

"What's the matter, sweetie?" Mum asked. "Are you missing us?"

"Yes," I said. "Can I come and stay with you? I'll help take care of Granny."

"Sweetie, Granny is doing great! She has the flu but she's feeling so much better."

"So can you pick me up right now?"

Mum laughed. I didn't find it funny at all.

I didn't want to stay with Angel anymore. Or her parents.

I missed my own family. I only missed Mum and Dad though, not my brother. He could stay with his friends forever.

"Mya, what's the matter?" Mum asked. "Does the best officer in the world need some help?"

"No, I'm okay...It's just hard. Angel is mean. Her parents have a big secret and we're trying to find out what it is."

"Sometimes parents keep secrets from kids because we don't want to upset you," Mum said. "I'm sure they'll tell Angel everything when the time is right."

"Maybe this case is too hard for me. Should I give it to another officer?"

Mum tutted.

"Mya, you can't give up and run away whenever things are hard...Do you need a boost? Something to keep you going?"

Mum's positive quotes were always a big boost. They made me feel much better when things weren't going well.

"Do you have a positive quote for me? I really need one right now."

Mum was quiet for a bit.

"Ah, I've got the perfect one. Listen closely."

Mum stopped to clear her throat. I held the mobile close to my ear, ready for her words.

"Successful people do what unsuccessful people won't do."

"What does that mean?"

"It means good police officers never give up. That's why they solve cases when others don't."

I wanted to be a good police officer who solves cases, so I couldn't give up! I would keep trying even though Angel's parents were good at hiding their sleepover secret.

"Mummy, thank you," I said. "I've got more work to do before I solve this case."

"We'll be ready to pick you up when the job is done. Good luck!"

After speaking to Daddy, I put my phone back on the bedside table and went over to Angel. She was still curled up in bed.

"Wake up!"

I shook her over and over until she finally opened her eyes. She groaned when she saw me and went back to sleep.

"Angel White, get up," I ordered. "If you want to stop your parents from divorcing, get up right now!"

She opened one eye and glared at me.

"I want to stop this divorce and get my grapes. You want to stop this divorce and keep your parents together. We'll both get what we want if you get up. You can't stop the divorce from your bed."

"Okay…" she mumbled.

We washed and got dressed before heading downstairs. As we walked into the kitchen, Angel stopped in front of me.

"Mummy?" she cried, running into the kitchen. "You're home early!"

Mrs White was pouring herself some coffee. There were huge bags under her tired-looking eyes.

"The first meeting was held early and the next two were cancelled," Mrs White said. She stopped speaking to let out a big yawn. "It's good to be home."

"Time for breakfast," Mr White said. "Choose your cereal, girls!"

We all sat down at the kitchen table. Angel's parents stuck to coffee. Angel and I had wheat cereal. Prince stayed under the table, his nose twitching.

Now Mrs White was back, I could finally solve the case! It was time to find the divorce papers.

My plan was simple. Angel and I had to check her mum's car. The divorce papers were probably hidden in there. If we got the papers, we could put them in the bin. Then her parents might forget the divorce and stay together forever.

But how could we get into Mrs White's car without her knowing? Easy! If she was really busy, she wouldn't notice Angel and I were searching her car.

How can we keep her busy? I thought. I know! Get her and Mr White to talk.

I thought they'd have a nice little chat. When they started talking, they wouldn't want to stop. Then Angel and I could sneak out to search Mrs White's car.

Unfortunately, their chat wouldn't go very well, and it would have a very smelly end…

Chapter 18

Mum and Dad loved talking to each other. Mum said she could talk to Dad for hours and hours if they had time.

But Angel's parents were different.

At breakfast, Angel's dad drank coffee while he stared into the garden. Mrs White drank coffee while she read her work folder. Angel stirred her cereal over and over, barely eating. Her teary eyes stayed on her mum, but why? I watched Mrs White to find out.

Angel's mum gave the meanest look to Mr White. It was the same mean look I gave to my brother when he ate the last chocolate in the fridge.

I ate my cereal, keeping an eye on everyone, even the dog. One minute, Prince was asleep. The next, he watched TV even though it was muted.

"Mya, your parents called," Mr White said. "Your grandmother is doing so well. You should be back home this weekend!"

He looked very happy about me leaving. Probably because he thought their secret divorce would stay a secret if I wasn't around. Well, he was wrong. I would NOT leave until the truth was out. A good police officer doesn't give up so easily.

At least Mr White was talking now. I just needed Mrs White to start talking too. Then Angel and I could leave them to chat while we searched her mum's car. The divorce papers might be hidden there.

The best way to get people talking is through "small talk". My parents did it at parties when they had nothing else to say.

I would use "small talk" to make Angel's parents speak to each other. But what small talk could we talk about first? Sports? Celebrity gossip? The news?

The news! That's an easy one to talk about. Every day something happens. The week before, an old man won the lottery. Fifty million pounds! My dad won the lottery once. He was so excited when he got the lottery email, but it said he'd only won two pounds!

He hasn't played since.

"What's on the news today?" I asked. "Can I put the volume up?"

"When we've finished eating," Angel snapped. "No television at the table."

"Good girl," her mum said.

Great! Angel just had to mess that up! I had to try again.

What else could we small talk about? Celebrities! There were lots of famous singers and actors we could talk about.

"Did you hear about the singer Shiny Star?" I asked Mrs White. "She got married to the rapper Jack Jones. He used to date the dancer Pamela Peters. She is best friends with the actress Jenny Brown. Shiny and Jack looked so happy on their wedding day!"

"Rappers don't have long careers, do they?" Mrs White said. "She'll end up supporting him when he runs out of money."

Mr White coughed really loudly. He gave Angel's mum a very mean look.

"What I meant to say was, who is Shiny Star?" Mrs White asked. "I've never heard of her. Is she very famous?"

"My parents and I do not waste time with

celebrity gossip," Angel said. "Besides, Shiny Star is a flop now. She only gets to number two on the charts. Sparkly Glitter is the best singer ever. All her songs get to number one."

"What do you think, Mr White?" I asked.

"Is Shiny Star the one with the pink glittery hair or is that Sparkly Glitter? I can't keep up! The charts change all the time."

"Change all the time," Mrs White said. "Just like your hair. And your job…"

The room went quiet again. Angel really wasn't helping me at all. Every time I tried to make small talk, she said something that stopped her parents talking.

Why can't Angel just keep quiet? I thought. Can't she see what I'm trying to do?

I should have told her about my small talk plan before trying it out. Would she have listened? Probably not. She was too busy brushing her curls a hundred times. She did it every morning, even before school. The only thing I did before school was wash, get dressed and eat breakfast.

Even though Angel was being a pain, I had to keep trying. So, what other small talk was there? The weather! People always liked talking about sunshine and rain.

"What's the weather like today?" I asked.

"The usual British weather," Mr White said. "Cold, rainy, and grey. We'll be lucky if we get any sunshine at all."

And back to silence we went.

By now I was running out of ideas. How much more small talk was there? I'd tried the news, weather and celebrity gossip. There was only one small talk topic left.

"Mr White? How's work?"

He froze. Mrs White almost choked on her coffee.

"Nothing to report," he said. "Still

working hard. Still earning lots and lots of money."

"Yes, his job is absolutely fine!" Angel's mum said. "Nothing wrong at all. We still have lots of money for Angel's presents, and we'll find a way to holiday this year."

"Find a way?" I asked. "What do you mean?"

"It's just very expensive," Angel's mum said. "The hotel, private beach, maids, chef, driver, babysitters, dog walker..."

"We can afford it," Angel said. "My parents earn more in one month than your parents earn all year." She stuck out her tongue!

Her mum mumbled, "*I* earn a lot..."

Her dad turned dark red and crossed his arms. "I earned, I mean I earn a lot too."

Uh oh. Small talk doesn't work when people are angry. I had to calm them down or one of them might leave the table.

"Nice day, isn't it?" I said. I looked outside and it started to rain. "Nice and, um, rainy."

Angel's mum nodded.

Her dad shrugged.

"Oh Andrew, please!" Angel's mum spat. "Do not shrug at the table."

"Where should I shrug? In the garden? In the bath? In the garage?"

"You can make that decision yourself," Mrs White said. "You seem to enjoy making big decisions by yourself."

"Like what?"

"You *know* what," she snapped. "And that red hair is…"

"Is what?" he cried. "I can't dye my own hair without your permission?"

"You keep making big decisions without consulting with us."

"I need to consult with my child to dye my

own hair?"

"When big decisions affect us all, you should!"

"Big decisions? Dyeing my hair is a big decision?" He slammed his mug on the table, wincing when the hot coffee spilt on his hand.

"Andrew, just be quiet!"

"No," he snapped. "Since I'm not allowed to shrug at the table, I've made the big decision to do *this* instead…"

Chapter 19

Mr White leaned to the side and let out the loudest, smelliest fart I've ever seen, heard or smelt. I pinched my nose and ran from the table. Angel ran upstairs after me in tears. Her parents argued at the table. They hadn't noticed we'd left. Or maybe they just didn't care.

Angel pushed past me and threw herself onto her waterbed. When I tried to give her a hug, she smacked my hands away.

My small talk hadn't worked, but now I had a better idea. I remembered the work folder Mrs White had. It seemed like a great place to hide divorce papers.

I had to get the divorce papers from the folder. Then Angel and I could hide them in the bin or bury them in the garden. Prince could help us dig a big hole. He dug lots of holes for his toys.

I had to be quick, though. Mrs White would leave for work soon. She might take the folder and hide it at the office, where I couldn't get to it.

When I left the bedroom, Mrs White ducked into the bathroom. She locked the door and wouldn't open it when I knocked.

"I need to talk to you," I said.

"I am, um, very busy right now!"

"I'll wait here until you come out."

"It might be a while…"

Good. I needed her to stay in there as long as possible.

I tiptoed downstairs and saw the work folder on a small table by the front door. I looked around for Mr White and found him in the living room, watching TV.

I'll take the work folder upstairs now, I thought. If he leaves the living room, I might not get another chance.

I dashed to the folder and picked it up. It was much heavier than it looked. I ended up huffing and puffing before I reached the stairs.

How many steps are? I thought. Sixteen? Oh boy…

Soon my arms were hurting. It got harder to hold the folder in my sweaty palms. Sweat trickled down my face as I puffed away.

Keep going, I thought. Twelve more steps…

Now my legs were tired too. They started wobbling as I took each step.

Eight more steps, I thought. But first I need a break!

"Prince, where are you?" Angel shouted from her room. "I need a hug!"

Prince's tiny feet pattered closer. He appeared from the kitchen and turned his head upstairs. Glaring at me, he showed his teeth. I showed mine back.

"Come here, boy!" Angel shouted. "Let's cuddle!"

Prince rushed upstairs, his eyes fixed on me. He was a small poodle, so there was lots of space for him to run past. Instead, he headed straight for me.

Before I could get out the way, Prince ran into my legs. He pushed his way through and rushed straight to Angel's room.

Meanwhile, I stood there trying to balance my wobbly body. I tried hard not to fall over while trying even harder not to drop the heavy folder.

"Hold on," I told myself. "Don't. Drop. The. Folder."

"Prince," Mr White called from downstairs. "Come for breakfast!"

Prince rushed out of Angel's room and leapt through the air. He banged into me, knocking the folder out of my hands. Hundreds of work papers flew everywhere.

"What on earth is going on out there?" Mrs White cried. "Never mind. I'm coming out!"

"Don't worry," Mr White said. "I'll check it out."

Uh oh, I thought. He's coming!

There were papers scattered all over the floor. I wanted to read them, but there wasn't enough time.

I grabbed as many papers as I could, trying to shove them back into the folder. Mr

White's heavy footsteps were coming closer and closer.

Hurry up, I thought. He'll be here any second now!

The kitchen door flew open and Mr White appeared. His eyes widened in horror when he saw the papers all over the stairs.

"Mya, what on earth have you done…?"

Chapter 20

"Well, Mya?" Mr White asked. "What're you doing with Bonnie's paperwork?"

"I…found it?"

"You found it all over the stairs?"

I nodded.

"Were you investigating again, Officer Mya?"

I nodded.

"Okay, let's fix this before my wife comes down. We'll both be in trouble if she finds out about this."

Mr White started picking up handfuls of

paper. He held the pages so I couldn't read much, but I did spot lots of numbers. They looked like the stocks and shares numbers I saw on the news.

Stocks and shares were numbers that went up and down. When they went up, people were very happy. When they went down, people were very scared.

It doesn't look like divorce papers, I thought. Is Mrs White's work folder really about work, or are they trying to trick me?

Probably a trick, I decided. Mrs White added fake numbers to some pages just in case Angel opened the folder. Then Angel wouldn't realise the other pages were about the divorce.

"What's the other stuff about?" I asked. I stood on tiptoes to get a closer look, but he held the papers close to his chest. "Why're you hiding it?"

"It's confidential. Sorry, sweetie."

"Confidential? Oh, you mean it's top secret! I'm not allowed to see it."

He quickly gathered the other papers and took them to the kitchen. I grabbed the folder and went after him.

Mr White spread the papers across the kitchen table and started putting them in order. Every time I got too close, he moved over, blocking my view.

"Mya, can you get some toilet roll from the cupboard under the stairs? Mrs White needs it. I forgot to change the roll last time I was there."

"I can help you sort out the papers!"

"I can handle this, thank you," he said sternly.

I crossed my arms and stepped closer to him. He wasn't getting rid of me that easily. I had a job to do and I would not quit just because things were hard.

Don't wish things were easier, my mum always said. Wish you were better.

"What does Mrs White do?"

"She's a finance lawyer. Very tough job. Very long hours hence all these papers."

"Do you work long hours?" I tried to peek around him, but he moved over. "You could go and get ready for work. I'll sort out the papers for you."

He paused for a moment before saying, "I'm not working today."

Or yesterday. He didn't seem to do anything! If he didn't do more work, he might get told off by his boss. When my brother got his first ever job, he was told off for being late five days in a row. Being late is bad, but not showing up is even worse.

"Will you work tomorrow?" I asked. "Or next week?"

"I don't work every day," he said. "I work whenever I want and earn whatever I want. Just like your dad."

I wanted to do the same thing when I was older. It'd be nice to work whenever I wanted and earn whatever I wanted. I'd spend twelve hours a day solving cases if I could. Hopefully I'd earn millions of pounds. Why? Because then I could buy millions of juicy, green grapes!

"You told me you're an Office Manager, remember?" I said. "How can you manage the office from home?"

"Well, I'm not an Office Manager anymore."

"So what job do you do now?" I asked.

His face went pale like he'd seen a ghost.

"Are you a lawyer too?"

I managed a peek at the papers while he was thinking, but only saw more numbers.

"I'm not sure what I am anymore." He glanced over his shoulder nervously. "Don't tell Angel..."

"Don't tell her what?"

"My job...I..." He shrugged and smiled. "Nothing. Forget I said anything."

He pushed the last paper into the folder and closed it.

"I'll leave this in Bonnie's car."

He ruffled my fluffy hair and walked outside. I followed him, my eyes on the work folder. He locked it in the car parked on the driveway. When he came inside, he left the car keys on the fridge where I couldn't reach them.

I had to get up there, but I couldn't when he was watching.

How can I get him to leave the kitchen? I thought. I've got an idea...

"I think I heard Mrs White calling you," I

fibbed. I rushed to the door and cupped a hand to my ear. "She said the toilet paper is finished. Can you go buy some more, please?"

"I didn't hear anything," he said. "Anyway, there's no need to buy more. I'll just get some from the cupboard."

"The one under the stairs? She said she checked it already and there's none left."

"We ran out already?" He sighed. "I know we have an extra person in the house, but we shouldn't run out *that* quickly."

"Mrs White sounded *very* angry," I said. "You'd better hurry to the shop or she'll be late for work!"

"Oh, great! Does she think I have nothing better to do?" He rolled his eyes. "Now she's got me on toilet paper duty!"

He pulled on his coat and stormed out the front door, slamming it so hard a picture fell off the wall.

I peeked through the letterbox and watched him marching off down the street. For a minute or so, I listened out for Mrs White. She hadn't left the bathroom yet. Angel was still upstairs. The dog was sleeping in the living room.

I had the kitchen all to myself.

Great, I thought. It's time to get those car keys…

Chapter 21

Mr White was out. Mrs White was in the toilet. Angel was in her bedroom. Prince was asleep in the living room. Now there was no one to stop me from getting those car keys!

I pulled over a chair from the kitchen table and made sure the backrest was against the fridge. Dad said that's the safest way to step on a chair.

Slowly, I climbed up and peered over the top of the fridge. I could see the keys but couldn't reach them.

"Goodbye, everyone!" Mrs White yelled.

"I'm off to work!"

Nooooo! I wasn't ready yet!

I got down and ran upstairs, squeezing past Mrs White on the way. She said goodbye and continued downstairs.

I pushed open Angel's bedroom door and found her sleeping in the hammock on the balcony. I ran over and shook her awake. Giving me a mean look, she sat up and smoothed out her frilly, pink dress.

"I was having a lovely dream," she said. "I dreamt that I was queen of the world. Everyone had to do as I say. It was SO amazing!"

"Call your mum," I said. "Quickly!"

"Why?"

"Because…Just do it!"

"I won't help if you don't tell me why," she said, crossing her arms.

"I think they're hiding the divorce papers

in your mum's work folder. The folder is in the car. If your mum takes the folder to work, we might never find it. Then we can't keep your parents together."

"How can we stop her from leaving?"

We looked over the balcony and saw Mrs White heading towards the car. She was holding the car keys.

"Cry," I said. "Just cry. Really loud. Keep her busy up here so she doesn't leave."

Angel cleared her throat and quietly practised crying. Then she opened her mouth and howled. It got louder and louder until I had to cover my ears.

When Mrs White heard Angel, she ran back inside and came straight upstairs. She put her car keys on the floor and hugged Angel.

"What's the matter, darling?"

"You...Daddy...Prince...Me..."

Angel howled again, louder and louder and louder. That's why her mum didn't hear me pick up the car keys and tiptoe out.

Now all I had to do was get outside and grab that folder. I had to be quick. Mr White would be back soon. If he caught me, he'd take the car keys away.

Quietly, I opened the front door and dashed down the garden path. I moved quickly so Mrs White wouldn't see me.

Suddenly Prince appeared at the front door. He growled at me and edged closer and closer. When I tried to shoo him back into the house, he barked.

"What's he up to down there?" Mrs White said. "Let me take a look, sweetie. Mummy will be right back, I promise."

I jumped into a rosebush just before Mrs White looked over the balcony. I managed to crawl deeper inside without getting scratched. It was hard because the thorns kept getting caught on my afro hair.

"Prince, stop chasing cats and get back inside!" Mrs White shouted.

Prince crept closer to my hiding spot, showing his sharp, white teeth.

"Prince David Jonathan White," she snapped, "ignore me again and you'll have no doggy treats for a whole month!"

Prince's fluffy ears flopped down. He hurried back into the house with his tail between his legs.

Angel was crying so loud I could hear her from downstairs. Mrs White started giving her lots of kisses and hugs, but it wasn't working. Actually, it seemed to make things much worse.

I peeked out of the rosebush and saw Mrs White looking my way. I froze, wondering if she'd seen me.

"Darling, please tell me what's wrong!" Mrs White turned back to Angel and gave her a big hug. "I can't help if you don't talk to me."

"Why?" Angel cried. "Mummy, why?"

"Why what?" Mrs White threw her hands up. "Princess, tell Mummy what's the matter!"

Angel ran into her bedroom and Mrs White followed.

I crawled out and pushed the biggest car key into the lock. It didn't fit. I tried another key. That didn't fit either. Finally, the last key slid inside, so I turned it.

The car alarm blasted my ears. I yanked out the key and crawled back into the bushes.

"What on earth?" Mrs White rushed out to the balcony. "It must be that cat again. It can't keep its paws off my car. If it leaves one more scratch I'll—"

"Mummy!" Angel shouted.

"Coming, darling!"

Mrs White went back inside and closed the balcony doors. I waited a moment, just in case she came out again. She didn't.

Get that folder, I thought. Hurry up before Mr White gets back!

I crept back to the car and pressed a big button on the key. The headlights flashed and the car bleeped. Then the car door opened by itself.

Cool…

And there it was. The work folder that was full of divorce papers. I grabbed it and pulled out pages from the middle. The middle is the best place to hide top secret stuff because some people read the beginning and skip to the end.

I flipped through the middle pages, but there weren't any divorce papers there. Just lots of writing about two businesses getting together in a "merger". Would someone really read through three hundred pages about something so boring?

Where is the divorce stuff? I thought. Where's the real divorce folder?

I opened the glove compartment and dug through lots more paperwork. Then I searched under the seats. I even climbed over the back seat and looked in the boot, but it was empty.

"What on earth?" Mr White cried. He dropped his shopping bags and ran over. "Why'd she leave the car open?"

I had nowhere to hide. It was too late to run. Mr White looked through the back window and saw me.

"Mya...?"

"I...I..." I couldn't think of a good excuse, so I sat there in silence.

"Mya, you kept watch over the car. What a good little police officer you are." He patted my head. "Don't worry. I'll lock up."

"But the work folder..." Maybe I should've checked the front and back too? "I, maybe, found it open..."

"Of course you did." He winked. "I won't tell if you don't."

We shook on it.

Mr White locked the car and we went back inside. I ran upstairs just as Mrs White came down. Her suit had snot and tears all over it. Even the dark grey suit couldn't hide the squidgy booger on her sleeve. Yuck!

Mr White pulled her into the living room and closed the door. I listened from the upstairs landing.

"Bon, are you crazy? You left the car open!"

"Did I? Anyway, Angel was distraught.

She thinks we're—"

"You can't leave the car open like that! I know we've got security cameras but still...Cameras won't stop someone from driving off in your car!"

Security cameras?

I looked at the ceiling and spotted a red light flashing in the corner. I hadn't noticed it before.

If I checked the cameras, I'd finally find out the truth. Her parents could hide from me and Angel, but not from the cameras.

Security cameras see everything! They must've recorded Angel's parents talking about their divorce. When Angel saw the tape, she'd finally accept that her parents had already divorced, and we were too late to stop it.

Hopefully Angel would still pay me ten thousand pounds. My stomach grumbled when I thought of all the juicy grapes I could buy. I'd get a shopping trolley full!

Angel came out of her bedroom and met me on the landing. We sat on the top step.

"Angel, you didn't tell me about the security cameras!"

"Why would I? It's a family secret. We can't tell just anybody about them."

"But I'm not just anybody," I said. "I'm the best girl police officer at school."

Angel yawned.

"Anyway, how many cameras are there? Where are they?"

Angel counted on her fingers before speaking.

"Eight cameras," she said. "There's one camera in the hallway and one on the landing."

"And the other six?"

"The living room, the kitchen, the dining

room." She stopped to think. "There's two in the back garden because it's so big. And one camera in the front garden, so we can see the driveway."

"Nowhere else?"

"No cameras in any bedroom or bathroom," she said. "That would be weird."

Angel sat against the wall, her face slowly turning red. She was very angry about something. It could've been anything. Maybe somebody moved her favourite hairbrush. Or someone left the lights on in her playhouse. Or maybe one of her curls wasn't as shiny as the others.

"Angel, what's wrong?"

"Mum said they're not getting a divorce."

"Do you believe her?"

"I think so…"

"So why're you angry, then?" I asked. "If your parents aren't divorced or divorcing, you should be happy!"

"But she still won't tell me what their secret is." Angel clenched her fists like she'd smack something. "If the secret's not a divorce, what could it be?"

"Are you sure it's not a new baby?"

"No way! One is enough, Mum said." She shuddered. "We only have three spare rooms. There isn't enough space for another child."

"You could always borrow Will."

"Who?"

"My big brother. You can keep him if you want. I'll take your new baby brother or sister."

"Didn't you hear what I just said?" She rolled her eyes. "I am enough. No more children!"

I wondered what else her parents could be hiding from her.

"Maybe a new pet?" I said.

"I wish it was," she cried. "Parents don't keep nice secrets for this long. It has to be something bad, not something fun like a new pet."

There was only one other bad secret I could think of.

"Maybe they're sick? Like my gran?"

For a second, Angel looked sorry for me. Then she shrugged and turned away.

"We're wasting time talking," she said. "If they told their secret on camera, let's get the video! The cameras record all day every day, even in the dark."

"Where do they keep the videos?"

"Under the stairs." She leaned in and whispered, "The password is Princess Angel."

Password? I wondered. Why did we need a password to go under the stairs?

At home, the only things we had under the stairs were the vacuum cleaner, some coats and shoes.

"Why is there a password for going under the stairs?"

"Don't ask," Angel said with a grin. "You'll find out soon..."

This was it. The moment we'd been waiting for. The cameras would show the secret her parents were keeping.

But we couldn't check the cameras now. Her parents were still downstairs, arguing with each other.

We had to wait, but only until early Friday morning. When Angel's parents were asleep, we'd sneak downstairs and watch the camera videos. At breakfast, we'd show her parents the videos. They'd have to tell the truth then.

Finding out the big secret wasn't the only great news! The camera videos were under the stairs. That meant we wouldn't have to go in the basement where evil spiders lived. I was very happy about that!

"What're you smiling about?" Angel asked.

"I'm glad we're not going into the basement, that's all. I hate all the dust, junk and spiders down there."

"Don't worry, Mya," she said, resting her hand on mine. "We won't be going into the dark, spooky, dusty, scary basement. I promise…"

Chapter 22

It's hard getting up early on winter mornings. Your bed is so warm and cosy. Instead of getting up, you pull the covers tightly around you and close your eyes for a few minutes longer…

But not today. I was so excited about the case that I got up straight away. I couldn't wait to find out what secret Angel's parents were keeping.

Angel was still asleep. Every time I woke her up, she rolled over and went back to sleep.

"I'll be going home this weekend," I whispered. "If I don't solve the case today, I might not get another chance…"

She got up straight away and grabbed a pretty bracelet from the bedside table. The bracelet had lots of tiny hearts and stars on it that jingled every time she moved.

We didn't leave the bedroom right away. I listened out for footsteps. I couldn't hear any. I also couldn't hear Mr White watching TV downstairs.

After a few minutes, we crept out and went to Mrs White's room. I pressed my ear against the door and listened closely. She was mumbling in her sleep.

"Put your bracelet on the door handle," I said. "Be very quiet! We don't want your mum to wake up and catch us."

Angel nodded. She quietly put the jingling bracelet on the door handle. I wanted it there so we'd hear Mrs White leave the room. If we heard the bracelet, we'd have time to hide under the dining room table.

Or we could pretend we'd gone down for a midnight feast. That's what Will said last week when he sneaked out to see his girlfriend. Mum caught him. She shouted at him so loud the neighbours across the street heard!

"Did you bring the squeaky dog toy?" I asked.

Angel handed me a plastic bag. Inside was a toy bone covered in dog spit.

No wonder she didn't want to touch it…

"Where should we put it?" she asked.

"Downstairs. It's too dangerous by the stairs. Your mum might trip on it and fall."

We tiptoed downstairs and stopped by the living room. I peeked inside and saw Mr White sleeping on the sofa. I quietly closed the door.

I placed the squeaky toy on the hallway floor. If Mr White came out of the living room, he'd step on the toy and make it squeak. If Mrs White came downstairs, she'd step on it too. Either way, Angel and I would have a squeaky warning that someone was coming.

Our plan would work as long as Prince didn't take the toy away. He liked sleeping in the living room, but moved upstairs if it got cold. If he went upstairs that night, he'd take the toy with him. Then we wouldn't know if Mr and Mrs White were nearby.

"We need to be quick," I whispered. "Your dad might wake up. Prince might take away his toy. Your mum might come downstairs for a drink."

"This won't take long," she whispered back. "We'll go in, watch the videos and go back to bed."

We both turned to the cupboard under the stairs. My hand was shaking when I reached for the door.

It's just a cupboard, I thought. Stop being a scaredy-cat!

I hoped it was just another boring cupboard under the stairs. All I wanted to see was a vacuum, broom, dustpan and brush, or maybe some coats and shoes.

But what if something really bad was in there…like evil spiders! They love hiding in dark, quiet spaces where they can build massive webs.

I wasn't just scared, though. I was also excited about checking security cameras again! The first time I ever checked cameras was in our headteacher's office. It was a naughty thing to do and I'm lucky I wasn't caught!

I hoped I wouldn't get caught this time either…

"I can't see anything," I said, looking around the dark cupboard. It was a bit spooky. So was the silence. It felt like someone had stuck their fingers in my ears.

"What's the password for?" I asked. "It looks like a normal cupboard to me."

"You'll see," she said. "Get in."

We got inside and Angel closed the door. I held my breath, feeling trapped. I wanted to leave but I couldn't run away. If I did, Angel would tease me about it forever.

"Angel," I said, my voice trembling, "I'm not scared or anything but…can you turn on the lights, please?"

Angel clapped once.

Bright lights lit up the cupboard.

"What do you think now?" Angel asked, grinning. "Does it still look like a boring old cupboard?"

No. There was something strange about it. It wasn't like the cupboard under the stairs at home. There was no vacuum cleaner and ironing board. Just a wonky shelf with a dusty can of baked beans on it. The food looked too old for anybody to eat without being sick. Besides that, the cupboard was empty.

The rest of the house had nicely painted walls and soft carpet that hugged your toes. In the cupboard, the brick walls were bare and dirty. There wasn't even a proper floor, just rough concrete so cold I could feel it through my bed socks.

"There's nothing in here," I said, trying not to sound disappointed.

Had Angel lied about the security videos? Maybe she'd tricked me? But why would she do that? Didn't she want to know the truth?

"Let's go back to bed," I grumbled. "I'll try something else later…without your help."

"What's wrong, officer? Are you sad because there's nothing in here?" She giggled. "That's what everyone thinks. That's what we *want* them to think…"

Angel pushed aside the baked beans can, revealing a red brick that didn't look as dusty as the others. She pressed the brick and the wall moved back slightly.

"Help me, Mya!"

Slowly we pushed the wall back until we saw a dark staircase leading down below. With a big smile on her face, she walked downstairs and left me behind.

I didn't want to go down into some dusty, old basement. There had to be hundreds of massive spiders in there with webs much bigger than me.

But I had to follow her. I didn't want to

stay in that tiny cupboard all alone.

"Wait for me," I whispered, hurrying down after her.

Downstairs, Angel was waiting for me under a dim ceiling light. Behind her was a metal door with a small black screen in the middle. She pressed her hand on the screen and it scanned her palm.

"Mya, you better keep this a secret or I'll...I'll...I'll be extra mean to you for the rest of the school year."

"That's seven more months!"

"Seven and a half, actually." She grinned. "Promise this secret room will stay a secret."

"I promise," I said out loud. In my head I thought, "I promise to only tell my parents, brother and very best friends."

Angel pulled out a card with her name and photo on it. She swiped it across the door's screen and stepped back.

"Princess Angel," she said.

After a loud bleep, the screen flashed and the door opened a crack. We looked at each other and smiled. It wasn't a friendly moment – we still didn't like each other – we were just glad the case was almost over.

"Go in," Angel said. "We don't have all day!"

"After you," I said.

It was *her* basement, so she should go first. Not because I was scared or anything...

Angel peeked inside and said, "It's safe to go in now. Come on!" She pushed the door open and went inside.

After a deep breath, I walked into the basement. I expected it to be cold, damp, dark, dusty and full of evil spiders. Instead it was light, clean and the strangest room I'd ever seen...

Chapter 23

Soon Angel and I would know what the big sleepover secret was. To find out the truth, we sneaked into the basement.

What a strange basement it was!

It wasn't cold, damp, dark or dusty. There were no spiders, cobwebs, mice, rats or bugs. This basement was shiny, clean, and so plain. The walls, ceiling and hard floor were all paper white. I couldn't see anything interesting like pretty paintings or colourful photos.

On the furthest wall were five long shelves

packed with food and water bottles. Below them were a widescreen TV and games console. There was also a sofa big enough for five people.

"Stand back," Angel said, elbowing me out of the way. "We've got work to do!"

Angel clapped slowly five times.

The room flashed. The staircase going upstairs slid into the wall and the door closed, locking itself. Now we couldn't get out!

Angel clapped three more times.

One wall trembled. It lowered down and a desk slid out. On it was a large desktop computer. It purred like a cat when the screen lit up.

On the computer screen were live videos from each security camera. I could see Mrs White's car parked on the driveway. Next, I checked the upstairs hallway. Luckily the bracelet was still on Mrs White's bedroom door. Then I looked at Mr White, who was still asleep in the living room.

I couldn't see Angel's dog anywhere.

"Where's Prince?" I asked.

"Who cares!"

Angel touched the screen and the videos rewound so fast everything was a blur. I saw the videos of myself over the past week. The cameras had recorded everything including my parents dropping me off, Angel falling into the pool, and me searching Mrs White's car.

"I wish we had cameras at home," I said. "It'd help solve so many cases!"

"You cannot afford security cameras." She looked down her pointy nose at me. "They cost thousands of pounds per camera, and that's just the black and white ones. Our cameras are ultra-high definition, wireless, digital, in full colour with a battery back-up.

We could have bought 3D cameras, but that would be showing off."

Yeah, THAT would be showing off…

Angel stopped rewinding the video when her parents appeared onscreen alone. They were in the living room. Her dad had a pillow and duvet on the sofa. If they weren't divorcing, why was he sleeping downstairs? The sofa was comfy, but not *that* comfy. Beds are always better because they're bigger and warmer.

"You ready to hear this?" I asked.

She pressed Play.

Angel's mum kept walking up and down, shaking her head. Angel's scruffy-looking dad was under the duvet, his arms behind his head. He was watching his wife, a grin on his face.

"Andrew, this is *not* funny! How could you do this to our family?" She stomped her foot. "Answer me!"

He sat up, still smiling.

"Bonnie, relax."

"Relax? Andrew, you have ruined our lives!"

He wasn't smiling anymore. Now his face was turning dark red.

"You want me to stay somewhere I'm unhappy?" He sighed. "I'm free, and it feels great."

"And what about how *I* feel?"

"I've been miserable for years so you and Angel could be happy." He stood up, looking taller than ever. "From now on, I'm doing me. You have to accept that."

"But—"

"But nothing!" He shrugged. "You'll have to manage on less money."

"And what do we tell Angel? She's not a stupid girl. Soon she'll figure out the truth!

Then what? How will she cope?"

"I coped just fine when my parents did the same." He spread his arms like he'd fly away. "I turned out all right, right?"

Mrs White burst into tears.

Angel stopped the video.

"We should play the rest," I said.

"What's the point? It's obvious they're talking about a divorce."

"It might seem obvious but we should hear the whole video just to be sure."

I reached out to play the video, but she smacked my hand away. I pulled my hand back and rubbed my sore skin.

"Angel, maybe they aren't divorcing?"

"So why is my dad sleeping downstairs?"

I wondered why I'd sleep downstairs.

"If you sleep downstairs," I said, "you might catch Santa leaving presents under the tree."

"That can't be the reason why he sleeps downstairs," she said. "Santa delivers our presents in a van. Delivery men carry the presents in and leave them under the tree."

I never knew Santa delivered presents that way. It was probably because the reindeers needed a break.

"Okay," I said, "maybe your dad sleeps downstairs because…because he doesn't want Prince to feel lonely."

"But Prince sleeps upstairs when it's cold. Dad stays downstairs every night, even when it's chilly."

"Well, maybe your dad stays downstairs because he falls asleep watching movies."

"My parents have a TV in their room. He doesn't have to watch the one downstairs."

I'd run out of ideas.

"Mya, if they aren't divorcing, why was my dad talking about being free?"

I wondered why I'd want to be free.

"Maybe now he works for free," I said. "My grandad works for free too. He called it volunteering. Volunteers aren't paid. That's why your dad said you'll have less money now."

Angel glared at me when I mentioned their money. She balled up her fists and looked like she'd bang something.

"They. Are. Divorcing," Angel spat. "I was right because I am smart. You are wrong because you are dumb."

I still wanted to watch the whole video. A good police officer hears and sees *all* the proof, not just bits of it, but I had no choice. My hand was still hurting from that last smack, so I let her turn off the video.

Then she just stood there, staring at me. I expected lots of tears, but didn't see any. If it was me, I would've cried like a big baby.

"Mya, my dad is moving out. That's why he changed his hair and clothes. He wants a new wife and a new baby."

"What about you and your mum?"

"He thinks we're old and boring," she said. "That's why he doesn't love us anymore."

Losing her dad like that would be hard. From now on he'd live somewhere else. He wouldn't be around to get rid of spiders, fix leaky taps, take her on bike rides, or fart at breakfast.

But she'd be okay.

I still didn't like her, but I'd be there for her. If she needed somewhere to stay, I'd find her a hotel. If she needed a cuddle, I'd call Prince over to hug her. If she needed anything else, she could ask her friends for help.

"You can cry, you know?" I said.

"I know that," she snapped. Her eyes were dry. "I am thinking."

"About who you'll live with?"

"No. My parents have pretended to love each other for weeks, maybe months."

"So?"

Angel turned to me, a naughty look in her eyes.

"Let my parents keep their secret," she said. "Let them keep pretending to love each other. As long as we don't say anything, they'll never know we know the truth."

"How long will they pretend for?" I asked. "Days, weeks, months, years?"

"Don't know and don't care," she said. "They can pretend forever. As long as they never divorce, everything will be just fine."

"But they aren't happy together!"

"Well, whose fault is that?" She crossed her arms and turned away from me. "I'll pay you tomorrow. Go to bed."

Ten thousand pounds. Wow. First, I'd buy Granny's medicine. Second, I'd buy thousands of green grapes. Third, I'd take my family on holiday somewhere hot and sunny. We'd leave Will over there, by accident. He'd find a new girlfriend and never come back.

Next, I'd turn Will's old bedroom into an office. He already had a desk, so all I needed were new pens and paper. Writing case files used up so much ink!

Soon it'd be time to write my report on the case. I'd say Mr and Mrs White were staying together. They'd pretend to love each other and, hopefully, never divorce.

"Everything will go back to normal," Angel said. "I'll have my old family back!"

I didn't think so.

Mr White would still sleep downstairs in the cold. Mrs White would still sleep upstairs all alone.

Mr White still wouldn't go to work and Mrs White still wouldn't stay home.

Mr White would still feel sad and Mrs White would still cry.

Angel's parents would argue more and more until they couldn't even eat together without farting…

But at least I was getting ten thousand pounds, right?

Right?

Wrong.

I couldn't do it. I couldn't pretend that everything was okay when it wasn't. I couldn't take the money knowing I'd left Mr and Mrs White feeling sad.

People had to come first, not money.

"Angel…"

"What?"

"I'm going to tell your parents we know

about the divorce."

Angel spun round and gave me the meanest, coldest, darkest look I'd ever seen. I was so scared I moved a bit closer to the door, even though it was still locked.

If she tried to hurt me again, I'd scream. We'd be caught by her parents and get told off, but she couldn't hurt me with them around.

"You will stay quiet," she hissed. "If you tell them the truth, I will pay you *nothing*. Yep! Not even one pence."

"But you promised!"

"Stay quiet, then. I want my parents to be together forever!"

"But they want a divorce!"

"Too bad," she spat. "I don't want two houses. I want one!"

She started pressing buttons on the computer screen. More videos of her parents popped up. She clicked each one and pressed Delete. I watched her delete the only divorce proof I had, but what could I do? The videos belonged to her family. If she wanted to delete them, it was her decision, not mine.

Angel typed in the password – it was Sweet Princess – and turned the screen away from me.

"I'm changing the password," she said. "You'll never guess what it is."

I didn't care what it was.

Her parents were unhappy together, but she didn't mind. Angel only cared about Angel. No one else mattered.

And that made me pretty mad!

I had to do something! I had to teach her a lesson! I had to fight back! I couldn't hit her because hitting people is wrong, but she wouldn't get away with what she'd just done…

Chapter 24

Angel wouldn't get away with deleting the videos. Now there was no proof that her parents were divorcing. It'd be her word against mine.

"You shouldn't have done that," I said. "Say sorry."

"Make me," she spat.

"I'm going to tell your parents what you did," I said. "Your crocodile tears won't work this time!"

"If you tell them anything, I'll…"

"You'll what?" I crossed my arms. "I'm not

scared of you!"

"I'll…I'll call your boss and complain. You'll lose your badge!"

"Do it," I said. "I'll lose my badge if it means your parents can be happy."

"They're happy already."

"They're *pretending* to be happy so you won't be upset," I said. "They're hiding the divorce because they love you. You don't love them, though, do you?"

Angel's eyes narrowed.

"Take that back."

"Make me," I spat.

Angel went to the shelves packed with food and drinks. Her eyes stopped on the water bottles. She grabbed one and splashed me. I snatched the bottle and splashed her back. She screamed and ran, so I chased her around the room.

"You wet my favourite pink nightie," she

cried. "Do you know how much this cost? I'm gonna get you for this!"

Angel slipped past me and grabbed two water bottles. She squeezed them and water flew out. It sprayed me, soaking my hair. Dripping wet, I squirted her right back, soaking her curls. We kept splashing each other until the bottles were empty.

Now we were soaking wet, but it didn't matter. Angel had her own bathroom, so we could dry our clothes in there. Her parents would never know about this water fight unless we told them.

"Who won the water fight?" she asked. "Was it me?"

"It's a tie," I said. "We both won!"

"No, I think I..."

Angel's eyes widened like she was scared of something. I followed her gaze across the room to the computer.

The computer was hissing like a cat. The screen was flickering, on and off, over and over again. Then smoke started rising from the computer.

"What's wrong with it?" I asked.

Angel pointed at the puddle on the desk. That's when I realised the whole computer was dripping wet.

"We wet it," I said. "Does it still work?"

"We'll get hurt if we touch it now. Electronics and water don't mix, Daddy said." She looked around the room. "There must be a towel we can throw over it."

She searched on one side of the basement while I looked on the other.

There were many plastic boxes packed away. Inside were useful things like a kettle, a blanket, a mobile and a torch. Why were they in the basement? And why did they all look brand new?

"Why is all this stuff down here?" I asked.

"For emergencies," she said. "If bad guys come into our house, we can hide down here until the police save us."

I went back to looking for a towel. Instead, I found something much more interesting. It was a big, red button on the wall. It said PANIC on it.

"Angel, what's this button do?"

She was digging through a box of pretty pink dresses. She barely looked at me when I spoke.

"Can I press it…?"

"Ooh! I haven't seen this dress in months." Angel twirled around. "Mum almost gave it to charity, but I didn't want to. I cried and got to keep it!"

"Can I press this button?" My hand touched the cold, hard button. "You sure?"

She nodded. "Of course I'm sure! It's

definitely the same dress. Mum spilt glitter on it. Very careless, Daddy said."

I should've stayed away from the button and kept looking for the towel. I shouldn't have pressed it without knowing what it did.

I pushed the button anyway.

An alarm blasted my ears. A metal door slid down from the ceiling, covering the basement door. This new door had no handle, keyhole or lock.

Lights popped out of the walls, flashing bright red. Angel was screaming at me, but I couldn't understand what she was saying. Then she started running around like a dog chasing its tail. Watching her made me dizzy, so I closed my eyes and wished it was all over.

Still screaming, Angel ran around in bigger circles until she knocked into the desk. Sparks shot out of the computer. The screen fell over, making the glass screen smash into tiny pieces.

Angel backed away in horror, heading straight for the wall.

"Watch out," I screamed.

Too late. She jumped from fright and banged into the wall. She threw herself out of the way just before the shelves fell down. Food cans, water bottles and boxes crashed to the floor.

With sparks flying, puddles everywhere, broken shelves, shattered glass, and a red-faced Angel glaring at me, all I could think of was my parents. I knew when they found out what I'd done, I'd be grounded for the rest of my life…

Chapter 25

It felt like we were stuck in the basement forever. I kept hoping the flashing red lights and loud alarm would stop, but they kept going and going and going...

Suddenly the flashing lights turned off. The loud alarm stopped, but my ears kept ringing for a while.

The thick, heavy door slid up into the ceiling where we couldn't see it. The other basement door unlocked and four police officers came in. Angel's parents squeezed past them and ran over to us. After planting lots of kisses on Angel's cheeks, they gave me a big hug.

"We thought someone kidnapped you," Mrs White said, crying her eyes out. "What're you doing in the panic room?"

"We came to see the cameras," Angel said.

"But why?" Mr White asked. "The basement is for emergencies only."

"Emergencies like what?" I asked.

"Emergencies like bad guys breaking in to steal our possessions," he said. "We could hide down here to keep safe."

"Hide down here?" I asked. "Is that why there's lots of food and water?"

"There's enough to last up to four weeks," he said, "but I'm sure we wouldn't be down here *that* long."

"How would you know it's safe to leave?" I asked. "What if the bad guys were hiding upstairs somewhere, waiting for you to come out? You'd be caught!"

"The cameras, duh!" Angel cried. "We'd check them to make sure the bad guys had really gone. When the police came to save us, we'd see them on camera and know it was safe to go out!"

"Exactly," Mr White said. "Now, young ladies, I have some questions for you."

Uh oh…

"Why do you want to see the cameras?" he asked.

"I lost my dolly somewhere," Angel fibbed. "If I check the cameras, I can see where I left her."

"That's not true," I said.

"Mya, is there something you want to tell us?" Mr White asked.

I was fed up with all the secrets. Angel's parents were keeping secrets from us. We were keeping secrets from them. All the secrets had made things much worse than they had to be.

So, I told the truth. Police officers, and everyone else, should just tell the truth. It makes things much easier.

"We saw the video of you talking about your divorce," I said.

Mrs White hugged Angel, rocking her like she was a baby.

"Princess, I told you already. We are NOT getting a divorce!"

"But Mum," Angel said, "Mya said you told her you've already divorced!"

"I *never* said we'd divorced!"

That was true. Mrs White never said they'd divorced. I just assumed that's what she meant.

It's a bad idea to assume or guess what people are thinking because you might be wrong...Was I wrong now?

"Are you sure you're not divorcing?" I asked.

"Definitely not," Mrs White said. "What made you think that?"

I stopped for a moment to think. As a police officer, I had to show them proof that I was right.

"Mr White sleeps downstairs," I said. "Why? He should sleep upstairs with you!"

"Yes, I've been sleeping downstairs recently, but it's not because of a divorce," Mr White said. "I stayed up late on my computer looking for...She can't sleep when I'm typing away. And the light from the laptop's screen doesn't help."

"I saw what you were looking for," I said. "Jobs and houses. You want a new house so you can move out and live by yourself."

"I was looking for jobs but…" Mr White rubbed his throat like it hurt. Mrs White gently pushed him aside and started talking.

"Mya," she said, "sometimes Mums and Dads sleep in different rooms. We did it this summer during the heatwave. I love the heat but he hates it."

"It was cooler downstairs," Mr White said. "And I got to sleep in the living room with our 63-inch, high definition television with surround sound speakers."

"And I got to sleep in peace and quiet." Mrs White took her husband's hand and squeezed it. "Some Mums and Dads sleep in different rooms. It doesn't mean they don't love each other. It's just that people sleep differently. I prefer darkness and silence. He prefers falling asleep while watching cat videos online."

"I knew that," Angel lied, "but Mya said that when parents argue a lot, they divorce."

"Not always, darling," Mrs White said.

"Sometimes parents don't get along. Sometimes kids don't get along either. Remember the time you and Cousin Agatha argued over the last crumpet? One argument didn't ruin your friendship, did it?"

"Yes, it did." Angel crossed her arms. "I still hate her. A lot."

I don't know why, but her parents laughed. It was strange because Angel obviously wasn't joking. She looked really angry. I guess it must've been a really tasty crumpet, not that I'd know. I hadn't eaten a crumpet before.

I did have a scone once. It was nice...

I showed Mrs White the divorce signs article Angel had printed. She looked over it with a sad look on her face.

"I see now," she said. "Mya, you can't believe everything you read online."

"But Angel is the one who found it," I

said. "She's the one who thought you were divorcing, not me."

"That's not true," Angel snapped. "I knew everything was okay."

"You're fibbing! Everything is NOT okay!"

I took the divorce signs article and pointed at the last paragraph.

"No more romance," I read aloud. "It says that if your parents don't kiss or hug, they don't love each other anymore. That's why your dinner date didn't work out."

"We do kiss and hug but not all the time," Mrs White said. "That doesn't mean we don't love each other. We show our love in other ways. You'll understand when you get your first boyfriend."

Yuck! I didn't want a boyfriend. Daddy said I shouldn't have one until I was at least thirty years old.

"Besides," Mr White said, "our dinner date went fairly well. We signed some important contracts, and the cereal was delicious!"

Wait a minute, I thought. They signed important contracts? They must've been the divorce papers!

"You signed some papers?" I asked.

"Yes…" Mr White started rubbing his throat again. Mrs White turned a bit pale. This time she didn't step forward to speak.

"What were the papers about?" I asked.

"Nothing," Mr and Mrs White said quickly.

"You're hiding something," I said.

Angel's parents looked away.

"See, Angel? They're divorcing! Just look at the article and think about it."

Angel took the paper and read it. She nodded before glaring at her parents.

"Mummy, Daddy, this article sounds like you two." Angel pointed at the page. "It says that if your parents are divorcing, they spend lots of time at work. Mummy does that. She didn't before."

"I have been working more hours," Mrs White said. "Well, that's because—"

"Your mother has a big project to complete," Mr White said quickly. He leaned over and read the article. "Yes, I changed my look, but that's not because I found another wife. It's because I wanted a fresh start. New hair, new clothes, new…"

He started rubbing his throat again. He was definitely keeping a secret, but was it a divorce or something else?

"But Daddy, what about you arguing a lot? It says here that when parents divorce, they argue all the time or don't talk at all."

"Baby, I already told you sometimes

parents argue," Mrs White said. "We don't always get along. It doesn't mean we stopped loving each other. It just means we disagree on something, especially something stressful like…"

Mr White placed a hand on Mrs White's shoulder. She closed her lips tightly.

She'd almost spilt the beans! I thought. The secret will be out soon…

"Mrs White, you said something stressful is going on," I said. "Stress means you're finding it hard to manage something, like a tough test at school. What's stressing you out, Mrs White? You can tell us."

"Cut it out, Mya!" Angel cried. "They're NOT divorcing, okay? I don't care what their secret is."

"But—"

"Stop asking questions," Angel hissed. "Just shut up!"

Her parents looked sorry for me. It made me feel sorry for myself. I'd been so wrong about the divorce. I'd messed up the case, just like a bad police officer would.

If people thought all officers were bad and couldn't solve cases, they wouldn't call 999 for help. That meant they'd be in trouble, all alone. I didn't want that to happen!

Oh, and 999 is only for the British police. If you don't know your country's emergency number, you should definitely find out what it is!

Anyway…

If Angel didn't care what the big secret was, that was fine. *I* cared, though. I wouldn't leave the case unsolved.

"Mrs White, what about your secret work folder?" I asked.

"It's no secret," she said. "Two companies are undergoing an important merger. One company is owned by the De Benson family, who is reluctant to sell such a valuable asset in the current market. Their reluctance is most likely due to the highly volatile stock market."

I didn't understand what she'd said, so I just nodded my head while she talked.

"The other company is owned by one of the richest women in Britain, Miss Deborah Winnifred-Smith. If I do an excellent, brilliant, impeccable job, she may give me quite lucrative opportunities in the legal, financial and accounting arenas."

Now everyone, including the four police officers, looked really bored or totally confused.

Mrs White stopped to take a deep breath before talking again.

"Was that all clear enough, Mya?" she asked. "I tried to keep everything simple."

"Um, yeah…"

"Good. I need this work contract badly for two reasons," Mrs White said. "First, this merger is a once in a lifetime opportunity. I might not get another chance to work on such a major project.

"What's the second reason why you need this contract?" I asked.

"Because of the money…"

Mr and Mrs White glanced nervously at Angel. She didn't notice because she was too busy looking down her nose at me.

"See, officer? You were wrong!" Angel poked my afro. "I will make a formal complaint to the prime minister about you. Then you'll get kicked out of Britain!"

"They're keeping a big secret!" I pointed at the broken computer. "The day before I came, your parents talked about a secret on camera. We both saw it!"

Angel shook her head. "I saw nothing. I was blinking at the time."

"Fibber! Your dad said he wasn't happy and wanted to leave. Your mum said he ruined your family." I turned to Mr White. "You're keeping a secret about your job, and I know what it is."

Mr White turned whiter.

"You got a job somewhere else because you're moving out," I said. "Yesterday, I asked what your job is and you said you weren't sure. Why? Everyone knows what their job is!"

I pointed at the emergency phone on the wall.

"Prove me wrong, Mr White, I dare you. Call your boss! I want to ask him why you're at home every day."

Angel pulled her dad over to the phone and put it in his hand, but he didn't dial the number. The phone was shaking in his hand and his teeth were chattering. Mrs White was pacing up and down, sweat trickling down her face.

"Call your boss," I said. "Unless you can't..."

Angel hugged her dad but he wouldn't look at her. Her mum went over and elbowed his side. "Andrew!" she hissed. "No more lies. Time for the truth..."

Chapter 26

Mr White turned away from the phone. Mrs White had tears in her eyes. The police officers hurried upstairs, leaving the four of us alone.

"It's true, isn't it?" Angel cried. "You ARE getting a divorce!"

Angel fell to her knees and screamed. Her dad covered his ears. Her mum told her to be quiet.

Instead, Angel ran to the box of clothes and tipped it over. She tore her dresses apart and poured food over her shoes.

"Angel White, stop this instant!" her mum yelled.

But she didn't.

Angel ripped the lid off another box. She pulled out some toys and threw them about. Every toy she broke made me sad. A little girl somewhere could've had that doll. A little boy could've had that scooter. Some poor kids would've loved those broken toys.

But Angel didn't care. She broke it all into tiny pieces until I could barely tell what anything was. Soon the toys were a colourful pile of broken plastic with a couple of doll heads scattered about.

When Angel was done, she sat down and crossed her arms. She looked at her parents like she was waiting for something. An apology, maybe?

Whatever she was waiting for, she didn't get it.

"Angel Princess White," Mrs White screeched, "you are a spoilt little madam. I haven't been so disappointed in you since last Christmas. You opened everyone else's presents without asking!"

"You had bigger presents than me!" Angel snapped. "That's not fair."

Mrs White stepped closer to Angel. She towered over her, her angry eyes bulging. Mrs White's face turned redder than Mr White's hair.

Angel looked scared. Wet-your-pants scared. She looked at me for help, so I looked away. Sorry, but she wasn't paying me enough money to get involved. If Mrs White told my parents what had happened this week, I'd be in serious trouble too. And you know Angel wouldn't help me!

"I am *disgusted* by your behaviour," Mrs White cried. "For the past five years, your father has been miserable. He worked a horrible job with horrible people, just so he'd make lots of money to keep us happy!"

"So what!" Angel snapped.

"Wow…" her mum said, shaking her head. "Angel, how could you repay him with such incredibly embarrassing, terribly shameful, outrageously rotten behaviour?"

Angel stuck her fingers in her ears, so her mum raised her voice.

"Angel, your father and I are not getting a divorce."

Angel clapped. "I knew Mya was wrong!"

"Your father quit his job. He'll be working at home from now on."

Angel shrugged.

"Until his new business takes off, we'll live on a quarter of the income we're used to."

Angel's eyes widened. The tears were coming soon.

"Angel, we can no longer afford this big house. We're selling it."

"Mr White doesn't have a job?" I asked. "Is that why you're looking for smaller houses? And why Mr White spends all day looking for jobs? Because you have less money now?"

"Who told you we're looking for smaller houses?" she asked.

I couldn't tell her we'd been snooping around her bedroom and checked her computer. I had to tell a lie instead, even though lying is wrong.

"I heard you yelling when you argued," I fibbed. "You talked about houses and jobs…"

"Anyway, to save more money," Mrs White continued, "we'll only holiday once a year in England. We'll be selling our holiday homes in Jamaica, Australia and Spain."

Even Mr White looked surprised.

"Bonnie," he said, "we don't need to cut back *that* much."

"We don't, but after realising how spoilt our daughter is, spending less money will do her some good. Just look at this place. It's full of broken toys, broken shelves, and a broken computer…"

"But Bonnie, we planned for two houses, remember?" Mr White said. "A home away from home?"

"One home is all we need," Mrs White said. "Other families do just fine with one house. So can we."

Angel let out an even louder scream.

"I can't be poor!" she shouted. "Only one holiday a year? Do I have to share a bathroom? Argh! No fair!"

"Too bad," Mrs White said. "Anyway. Be happy that your daddy and I still love each other."

Her parents kissed and then hugged.

"What about the papers you signed?" I asked. "We thought you were signing divorce papers."

"No way," Mr White said. "Those papers were for the bank. They'll be lending me money. When I get paid, I'll be open for business."

"And be your own boss," Mrs White said happily. "I'm a bit jealous!"

I was too. Could I be my own boss? I'd love to have no boss telling me off. I could tell myself off instead.

"So Mrs White is working more because you aren't working?"

"Exactly," he said, "but not for long. Do you remember that phone call yesterday?"

"Someone in Switzerland."

"Smart girl." He ruffled my afro puff.

"Yes, well that is my first customer."

Mr White looked so happy. His eyes were glowing. Mrs White looked at him proudly.

I thought having no job was sad, but they looked happy about it. Now he had a better job than the one before. Something bad (quitting his job) led to something good (a better job). They had less money but more happiness.

Angel wasn't happy, though. She stood there, glaring at me through gritted teeth. Her fists were trembling by her side.

"Mr White?" a deep voice called from upstairs. "Is everything all right down there? Can we leave now?"

"The police," Mr White cried. "I'd forgotten they were here! Bonnie, let's go and explain everything. Girls, wait here."

Mr and Mrs White went upstairs to the police, leaving me alone with Angel. She kept glaring at me, an evil look on her face. I backed away, keeping a big gap between us.

"So, Angel, I helped you out...You're still paying me ten thousand pounds, right?"

She nodded, patting her nightie pocket.

"The money's here," she said. "Come and get it."

"Could you throw the money over to me?"

"I can't throw ten thousand pounds. It's too heavy." She took a step closer to me. "Come over here, Mya."

"Maybe post the money to me, then?"

"Mya, come over here and get your money! Now!"

Could she fit ten thousand pounds into her pocket? No way! That's too good to be true, so it had to be a trap.

A good police officer knows a trap when she sees one. People who set traps are usually mean, just like Angel.

"Come on, Mya. Don't be scared." Angel took another step closer to me. "Don't you want money for your sick granny?"

"Yes, but…"

Traps are really dangerous, especially when no one else is around to save you. Just like now. Her parents were chatting upstairs. They sounded so far away. If this was a trap, no one would be there to save me.

I'd be on my own.

"Come on," Angel said, stepping closer to me. "Think of all those juicy grapes. A million of them. You don't have to share them with anyone."

Too good to be true, I thought. I'd better run before she gets any closer!

But my grumbling stomach thought I should take a chance. Could I miss out on a million grapes? I stopped to think about it.

A good police officer is always focused on

the job, no matter what. Right now, I wasn't focused at all. My stomach was thinking about all those juicy green grapes at the supermarket...

While I was daydreaming about grapes, Angel lunged at me. She grabbed my pyjama sleeve and wouldn't let go. I pulled back, but she was too strong. I yanked my arm away and the sleeve tore.

Angel grabbed my sleeve with both hands and tugged. I pulled the other way, trying to reach the stairs.

"Get back here!" Angel hissed.

"No way!"

I took a deep breath, gathered all my strength and threw myself down. Angel fell forwards and bumped her head on the floor.

While she was rubbing her head, I pulled off my top and threw it over her head. Now I was in my vest and pyjama bottoms. At least she couldn't grab my sleeves anymore.

I ran upstairs. Angel's footsteps were close behind. Huffing and puffing, I didn't stop until I was back in the cupboard under the stairs.

I stepped into the hallway and heard Angel's parents chatting to the police outside.

If I reached them, I could have Angel arrested for being so mean to me. Being mean isn't against the law, but Angel didn't know that!

I dashed to the front door. I could see police officers standing by their car, its blue lights flashing brightly. Help was so close. I would've made it, but then I stepped on the squeaky dog toy...

Chapter 27

I was so close to the front door. Once I got outside, I'd scream for help. The police officers would rescue me because officers always help each other.

But before I reached the door, I tripped over Prince's squeaky dog toy. He must have left it there before going outside.

My foot slipped on the toy. I tumbled into the front door, accidentally slamming it shut. I reached up to turn the door handle, but Angel appeared and slapped my hands down.

"I'm an officer of the law," I yelled. "Put

your hands up and leave me alone!"

"This is my house," she yelled back, "and you're coming with me!"

"Angel, Mya, is everything all right in there?" Mrs White cried.

Angel put her hands over my mouth. "Just playing, Mummy!" she said. "We're going to bed now."

I managed to push her hands away, but when I opened my mouth to scream, she grabbed my ankles and pulled me back to the basement.

I couldn't let her drag me down there! No one would ever see me again! She'd bury me under the pile of broken toys. Then the toys and I would be dumped with the weekly rubbish. I'd live on a rubbish tip with seagulls and dirty nappies.

No way!

When she pulled me into the cupboard

under the stairs, I clapped. The lights went out. She clapped, turning them back on. With my ankles free, I could finally escape!

I jumped up and ran upstairs. Angel followed, chasing me into her bedroom. I rolled across the bed and landed on my feet. She followed me but banged into the bedside table.

"Why're you doing this?" I asked, huffing away.

"Because I hate you!" she said, puffing away.

"Why? Your parents aren't divorcing! You should be happy."

"I *am* happy about that, but I'm *not* happy about being poor like you." She edged closer, her narrow eyes fixed on me. "I got one hundred toys for Christmas last year. I might only get fifty this time."

"That isn't MY fault."

"I don't care," she spat. "I can't take it out on my parents, but I can take it out on you!"

Angel jumped at me but I side-stepped. She fell onto a chair, knocking the wind out of her. While she was gasping for air, I hid in the playhouse and closed the door.

"Come out!" Angel shouted. She banged on the front door, but I held it shut. "Mya, let me in! That's *my* house!"

No way! I didn't want to end up like the broken toys in the basement.

"I'm coming in whether you like it or not!"

She marched out to the balcony and pulled down the hammock. Her mum called upstairs, but Angel just ignored her.

"This is your last chance," Angel said. "Come out with your hands up, officer!"

"You want me to come out? Make me!"

Angel tied both ends of the hammock to

the balcony doorway. Now the hammock looked like a massive slingshot, but instead of shooting stones, she was going to shoot herself into the playhouse. If it worked, she'd fly into the house and knock it down. That would be fine if I wasn't still inside.

I had to get out!

I grabbed the door handle, but I turned it too hard. It broke off. The door wouldn't open. I was stuck!

"Help!" I yelled. "Somebody help me!"

Angel backed away, her bottom in the giant slingshot. She pulled back as far as she could, and then counted down from ten.

"Ten, nine, eight..."

I tried squeezing through the windows, but the flower pots were in the way. I tried to push them off the windowsill, but they were glued down.

"Seven, six, five..."

I climbed up the playhouse stairs and pushed against the heavy roof. It opened a crack, but only my arm could get through.

"Four, three, two..."

I got into the tiny playhouse bed and hid under the covers. I peeked out, my body trembling.

"One!" she cried. "Here I come!"

Chapter 28

Angel lifted her feet off the floor and the slingshot flew forward. It threw her out, but not very far. She fell over and landed face first in a tub of pink plasticine. When she looked up, there was a plasticine moustache stuck to her face.

I laughed. Maybe I shouldn't have...

Angel pushed away the plasticine tub and searched through a pile of toys on the floor. There was a dinner playset, so she grabbed the plastic knife.

"What're you doing with that?" I asked.

"Nothing…"

"Let's talk about this, okay?"

Angel climbed onto the playhouse roof and started using the knife to unscrew it. I had to do something quickly before she got inside.

I banged on the roof, shaking her about. She barely held on and the knife wouldn't stay in the screws.

"I never liked you, Mya," she said, banging the roof with her fist. "I'm going to tease you forever!"

"I don't care!" I banged on the roof again, almost knocking her off.

"You think you're so smart, but you're not. You're too dumb to be a *real* police officer!"

"Take that back," I said, my face burning. "I AM a real police officer. I have a badge and I've solved cases!"

"Your *toy* badge? Whatever! I saw that thing at the pound shop when I walked past. Of course I would never shop there. Everything is too cheap."

I know police officers are supposed to stay calm, but she made me so mad! First, she'd said I wasn't a real police officer. Of course I was! Police officers can be any age. Everyone knows that.

Second, she'd said my badge was just a toy. Yes, some kids used it like a toy, but I didn't. It was a real badge to me.

A real police officer isn't about wearing a fancy badge or uniform. A real police officer cares about people and solves cases. I cared about people and solved cases, so I was definitely a real police officer. It didn't matter what Angel said. She didn't matter to me anyway because I didn't like her.

I also didn't like how she'd bashed pound

shops. You can get some great stuff there. Not everyone had lots of money like her…or like she used to.

"You're not the richest girl at school anymore because your dad doesn't have a job. You have less money now, so you'll be shopping at the pound shop soon!"

"You take that back!" she screamed. "Take it back right now!"

"Make me!"

"I'm going to get you," she said. "And then I will take your badge and…" She giggled.

Angel unscrewed faster, her face turning dark red. I tried shaking the roof again, but she just thumped it back down with her fists.

She lifted the roof a bit, her narrow eyes on me. I started to sweat, my teeth chattering. She reached inside with one hand and grabbed my hair. Her other hand was holding on tightly to the roof.

I tried to wriggle free, but she kept tugging my hair.

"You're hurting me," I cried. "Let go!"

"Make me!"

I reached up and shoved the roof as hard as I could. Half the screws popped out. The roof tipped over. Angel was thrown off. She flew, the plastic knife still in her hand. Below her was the waterbed.

You know what happened next...

Chapter 29

Angel flew off the playhouse roof and headed straight for the waterbed. She held her hands out, the knife pointing at the bed. A second later, she landed with a thud.

Bang!

The knife popped the waterbed. Water flowed out and spread across the floor, soaking all her toys and schoolbooks.

"Are you okay?" I asked.

Angel opened her mouth to speak but no words came out. She sat on the flat, empty waterbed without moving. Her curls were all straight and dripping wet. Her eyes were wide open in shock.

"Angel!" Mrs White shouted upstairs. "What on earth is going on up there? Why is the ceiling leaking downstairs?"

Uh oh...

I had two options to choose from.

One, I could make sure Angel was all right. I'd wait for her parents to come upstairs and tell them what happened.

Or two, I could run and hide. I was pretty dry. It'd look like I was never there...

I didn't know what to do, so I ran down the hallway into Angel's bathroom. In there, I had time to think about whether I'd help Angel or not.

I locked the bathroom door and turned on the shower so no one would walk in. I stayed in there, thinking about the right thing to do, even when Mrs White ran upstairs and started yelling.

"Angel, are you crazy?" her mum shouted. "Look at your room!"

"You know why she did this," her dad said. "It's because she's not getting a hundred presents this Christmas!"

"Definitely not," Mrs White said. "Did you see what she did in the basement? It'll cost THOUSANDS to fix and replace everything."

"Did I see the basement?" He laughed. "How could I miss it? The place was a mess, but this is even worse!"

"Poor Mya," Mrs White said. "I think she's hiding in the bathroom. Angel, you are two months older than her. You should set a much better example!"

Angel screamed.

"That's it, young lady," Mrs White shouted. "We're giving away all your old toys. They take up three whole guest rooms. Ridiculous! You only played with them two or three times."

Angel screamed again.

"Would you like us to give away your Christmas presents too?"

Angel kept her mouth shut.

"Good," her mum said. "Now clean up this mess!"

While Angel cleaned her room, I stayed in the bathroom. It was nice to get away from the shouting and screaming. The quiet bathroom reminded me of home. The Whites were a very, very noisy family compared to us.

"Home sweet home," I said. "I can't wait to be back!"

I thought we'd go home and everything would be normal again. At home, I'd see Mum and Dad, not Mr and Mrs White. At home, I'd argue with Will, not fight with Angel. At home, my cat would cuddle with me, not growl like Angel's dog.

I didn't want Angel's life anymore.

I wanted my own life back.

It'll be okay, I thought. I'll be home soon.

I thought my family would have a nice, quiet day together. Just the four of us and a good movie. Nothing special. Just the usual stuff we did on the weekend.

Little did I know that my parents had not one but *two* big surprises waiting for me…

Chapter 30

"Welcome home," Mum said. "It feels good to be back, doesn't it?"

Will and I rushed out the car and ran into the house. I gave our cat a quick hug before going upstairs.

Seconds later, I pushed open the door to my bedroom. It was much smaller than Angel's, and I didn't have as many toys, but it was my room and I loved it.

Mum was right. It felt good to be back home. My house. My bed. My parents. All mine! My house felt so tiny when I thought of Angel's massive place, but so what? I had a lot less stuff than her, but I saw my parents a lot more.

"Kids, come downstairs," Mum said. "We need to talk."

My whole family sat at the kitchen table. Mum took my hand and Dad took Will's. I started feeling nervous. Was some bad news coming?

Maybe Granny was still sick? If she was, I couldn't buy her medicine because Angel hadn't paid me.

"Kids," Dad said, "we have some news about your grandmother…"

Footsteps shuffled closer to the kitchen. Our cat Iam started purring, his eyes on the kitchen door. We all turned to see who was coming in…

The door opened and Granny walked in very slowly. She had a walking stick to lean on. Grandad stayed right behind her, his hand resting on her back.

Granny's dark brown skin was pale. There were bags under her eyes, and her wrists were really thin. Her favourite flowery dress looked huge on her. It used to be a bit tight in the tummy area.

Will and I stood up so our grandparents could sit down. Will wrapped his arms around Granny while I sat on Grandad's lap.

Grandad was skinnier too. Probably because he was busy taking care of Granny instead of eating. Luckily his big belly was still there for me to tickle. I tickled him until there were tears in his eyes.

"Mya, we'll have a tickle competition later," Grandad said, trying not to laugh. "Your grandma has something very important to say."

"William, Mya," Granny said, "I'm going

to be just fine! I knew that flu couldn't beat me. I'm too tough!"

"Thank God!" Will said. "I thought you were gonna di—"

"William!" Mum wagged her finger. "Please don't say that."

"So, Gran's cool now?" I think I saw a tear in Will's eye. "Good. Well, I'm out. Got homework to do."

"You had entire week to finish your homework," Mum said. "What were you doing instead?"

"Well, Dave and me had a party...then Craig and me went to the cinema...then Allison and me—"

"William!"

He tried to run off, but Mum grabbed him by the collar and pulled him back into the kitchen.

In a huff, Will sat with his arms folded

while Mum told him off. Grandad told him off too. Then Mum told him off again. They kept taking turns while Will sat there staring out the window. He was probably thinking of his girlfriend...

Meanwhile, Granny told Daddy off because he'd left his dirty, oil-stained overalls in front of the washing machine. They'd been lying there for five days. Now the oil stains had dried and Granny couldn't get them out. She kept wagging her finger at Dad while he sat there staring out the window. He was probably thinking of his car...

There was so much yelling in our kitchen, but I didn't mind. Mrs White said adults argued sometimes, just like kids. Arguments didn't always mean something bad like a divorce.

That got me thinking...What if my parents divorced someday? What if they didn't love each other anymore?

I would be very upset. My life would change forever. If my parents didn't want to be married anymore, they'd live in two different houses. Will and I would split holidays and birthdays between our parents. One day, they might marry someone else. They might even have another baby…

But if they wanted a divorce, I'd be happy for them. Why? Because whatever made them happy made me happy too. Being happy apart was better than being sad together.

A happy family. That's what really mattered. Not cars, toys, holidays or a swimming pool. None of that made people happy. Mr and Mrs White had shown me that.

I didn't have three spare rooms. I didn't have a massive garage. I didn't have holiday homes. I didn't have enough dolls to fill a toy store. I didn't have Angel's life, and I didn't want it.

I didn't have what she had.

She didn't have what I had.

What do I have? I wondered.

I had grandads who took me to theme parks, and grandmas who cooked amazing meals. I had a dad who could fix anything in the world, and a mum who made very sick people better. Best of all, I had a brother who loved me, even though he never said it. He showed it though, every time he helped me.

I wouldn't swap my family for all the toys in the world. I wouldn't swap them for a billion juicy, sweet, bouncy, tasty grapes either. I wouldn't even swap them for ten thousand pounds. Family was more important than money. Angel's mum told me that when we spoke earlier.

"Mrs White," I said, packing my suitcase, "will you miss being rich?"

"Sometimes I will, sometimes I won't," she said. "Money has done amazing things for our family. It's paid for exciting holidays, amazing cars, the finest clothes and so much more, but…"

"But what?"

"But money also led to terrible things. Andrew kept a job he hated just to make more money. I worked away from home and missed so much, just to make more money. Because we focused on money, we didn't notice what happened to Angel…"

"What happened to her?"

"She became a spoilt rotten child. All because we bought whatever she wanted." Mrs White shook her head sadly. "It's our fault. We should've spent *less money* on her and *more time* with her."

Mrs White looked sad for a moment.

"Andrew quitting his job was a *good* thing," she said, smiling a little. "Earning less money means we can't spoil Angel anymore. Having less money and fewer things will show her what's really important in life."

"And what's that?" I asked.

"Family and friends," she said. "They're more important than money. They always have been and always will be."

She looked at their family picture on the wall. A big smile spread across her face.

"We're not rich anymore, but at least we have each other. Money comes and goes. Family stays forever."

She was right.

"Mya, are you okay?" Grandad asked. "Looks like you're daydreaming, as usual."

"I'm fine," I said. "Just thinking about this morning."

"You'd better think about the tickle competition, too," he said. "I've been practising my tickling skills on Granny. She said I'm pretty good at it now. Much better than I was before."

"You sure about that?" I said with a grin. "I've beaten you ten times in a row!"

"Ten times?" He raised an eyebrow. "How many times have I won?"

"Zero times."

"Oh…"

Poor Grandad.

Soon my other grandparents, cousins, aunts and uncles would come over to stay. Together, our family would all be happy and healthy on Christmas Day.

We didn't need lots of presents.

We didn't need lots of money.

We just needed each other.

CASE CLOSED

Dear Reader

Hello, I hope you enjoyed my book. You can email me at contact@zuniblue.com. I'd love to hear from you!

I'd really appreciate it if you left a book review saying whether you loved it, hated it, or thought it was just okay. It doesn't have to be a long review. Thank you very much!

Keep reading to get your 100 free gifts...

About the Author

Zuni Blue lives in London, England with her parents. She's been writing non-fiction and fiction since she was a kid.

She loves telling stories that show how diverse the world is. Her characters are different races, genders, heights, weights and live with various disabilities and abilities. In Zuni's books, every child is special!

Solve More Cases

Would you like to read another case file?

Mya doesn't share her cases with just anyone, but she knows she can trust you.

Keep reading for more top secret cases she's solved…

The Fat Girl Who Never Eats

Ten school burgers were stolen. Everyone blames the fat girl, but no one saw her do it. Is she the burger thief or is it someone else?

To solve the mystery, Detective Dove must face her crafty dad, a strange caretaker, and the shocking secret in the school basement...

The Mean Girl Who Never Speaks

There's a new girl at school. She never speaks, never smiles and never plays with other kids. Does that mean she's mean? Maybe. Maybe not...

To solve the mystery, Detective Dove must face a suspicious teacher, the school bully, and the meanest boss in the world...

The School Pet Who Went Missing

Mya's school has a brand new pet. It's cute, cuddly and loves everyone. Unfortunately, it's gone missing! Did it run away? Or was it stolen?

To solve the mystery, Detective Dove must face her bossy headmaster, a mean prefect, and a sneaky teacher with a dark secret...

The New Boy Who Hears Buzzing

The new boy's ears are buzzing. He must've been bugged, but who did it? Was it a student? A teacher? Or some bad guys?

To solve the mystery, Detective Dove must face the detention kids, a crafty inspector, and some naughty officers at the police station...

Dedications

This book is dedicated to anyone with family problems. Always remember: the perfect family doesn't exist.

Thank you to my family and friends. I appreciate all the love and support you have given me. I couldn't have done this without you.

An extra special thank you to every reader who's emailed me. I love hearing from you!

100 Free Gifts For You

There are 100 FREE printables waiting for you!

Certificates, bookmarks, wallpapers and more! You can choose your favourite colour: red, yellow, pink, green, orange, purple or blue.

You don't need money or an email address. Check out www.zuniblue.com to print your free gifts today.

Made in the USA
Columbia, SC
22 April 2020